Lavinia Howe Phelps

Dramatic Stories

For Home and School Entertainment

Lavinia Howe Phelps

Dramatic Stories
For Home and School Entertainment

ISBN/EAN: 9783337334918

Printed in Europe, USA, Canada, Australia, Japan

Cover: Foto ©Andreas Hilbeck / pixelio.de

More available books at **www.hansebooks.com**

DRAMATIC STORIES

FOR

HOME AND SCHOOL ENTERTAINMENT.

BY

LAVINIA HOWE PHELPS.

"A good deed is the only vessel that will hold a heavenly joy."— Rev. C. Giles.

CHICAGO:

S. C. GRIGGS & COMPANY.

1874.

PREFACE.

———

THIS book is presented to the young, irrespective of the *years* they have lived, with the hope that it may afford them many an evening's pleasant entertainment.

L. H. P.

CONTENTS.

"In all the plans of education, the main point is, that it should be a beatitude !   *   *   *   *   *

"All literature, art, science, are vain, and *worse*, if they do not enable us to be glad — *glad justly !* " — RUSKIN.

"Truths are introduced into the memory by their pleasures and delights." — SWEDENBORG.

"The highest use of art — in its dramatic illustrations of truth — consists in working out a recreation and a joy."

"I don't like to read about things, I like to *see* them," said Betsey Brown. "If Sally Grumble has a Christmas tree full of nice presents, I should like to *see* it ; and if grandma has a 'golden wedding,' with a wreath of orange flowers over her gray hair, I should like to *see* that too."

You are a wise girl, Betsey Brown. *Seeing* is more satisfactory than hearing. Invite a company of friends to visit you, then play "The Game of Nuts," and you can *see* poor Sally's joy when she learns she has friends ; and a little playful ingenuity will introduce to your parlor, grandma with her gray hair wreathed in orange flowers.

THE MANTLE OF CHARITY.

Characters:

MARY MORN,	MRS. HILL,
ANNA TIBBETS,	BENNIE, *her little Son*,
ELSEY GREEN,	SHERIFF.
CARL GREEN,	

MARY MORN and ANNA TIBBETS. (Mary is sorrowfully examining
a large picture she holds in her hand.)

ANNA. Mary, there is no question about the wicked
girl that spoiled your picture. I would go immediately
and show it to the teacher, and have her disgraced.

MARY. No, Anna, I will not do that; I will just lay
my picture one side and let it rest till after the examina-
tion, then begin a new one. I do not care about the
prize, but I do care about having a perfect picture, for
I intend to make a Christmas present of it.

ANNA. You ought to expose Elsey. If she had
daubed my picture over as she has yours, I would pull
every hair out of her head. I would never forgive her.

MARY. Anna, do you remember those sweet lines
of the poet?

"Think gently of the erring!
Ye know not of the power
With which the dark temptation came,
In some unguarded hour.

13

Ye may not know how earnestly
   They struggled, or how well,
Until the hour of weakness came,
   And sadly thus they fell.

"Think gently of the erring!
   Oh do not thou forget,
However darkly stained by sin,
   He is thy brother yet;
Heir of the self-same heritage!
   Child of the self-same God!
He hath but stumbled in the path
   Thou hast in weakness trod.

"Speak gently to the erring!
   For is it not enough
That innocence and peace have gone
   Without thy censure rough?
It sure must be a weary lot,
   That sin-crushed heart to bear,
And they who share a happier fate,
   Their chidings well may spare.

'Speak kindly to the erring!
   Thou yet may'st lead them back,
With holy words, and tones of love,
   From misery's thorny track.
Forget not thou hast often sinned,
   And sinful yet must be —
Deal gently with the erring one,
   As God hast dealt with thee."

ANNA. The poetry is very pretty, Mary; but poetry and practical life are two things.

MARY. We make them so — but they should be one. Think what a heaven we would have on earth if this beautiful poem of Miss Fletcher's lived in the hearts of the people!

ANNA. Thinking kindly of the erring would not turn

them from their errors. Speaking kindly to them would not save them from rushing madly downward to meet the hellish troupe waiting to receive them.

MARY. It would do much to keep them back, Anna: love, and charity the form of love, has a mighty power; but the world has not faith in it. When a weak brother or sister falls, how often do we see the world set its heel upon them and hold them down. "Beelzebub can never destroy Beelzebub."

ANNA. But a stronger Beelzebub can keep a weaker one under control.

MARY. Yes, that may be; and that is the limit of the dark one's power. How different is the office of charity! It gently binds, while it gives freedom; it forces no control, but it imparts of its own beautiful life an influence that helps to change desire.

ANNA. Your words sound musical, Mary. I feel an influence from your life that I do not understand. There is a great difference between us. As I said about Elsey, if she had daubed my picture as she did yours, I would pull her hair all out of her head. I would n't stand it.

MARY. If Elsey were the one that spoiled my picture

———

ANNA. You need not say if she were the one — everybody knows she was the one.

MARY. I do not like to believe it.

ANNA. But your picture is spoiled, and some wicked hand spoiled it. Why not believe it of Elsey as easily as of any one else?

[*Enter* ELSEY GREEN.]

ELSEY. Mary Morn, I heard your picture was spoiled;

is it true? [*Mary unrolls her picture.*] O, that is too
bad! Your picture was so perfect. I have watched
its progress daily, and admired your delicate shading.

ANNA. We all know you have watched its progress
daily. I suppose now the gold medal will be yours; but
it rightly belongs to Mary, as the whole school knows.

ELSEY. Yes, it belongs to Mary; but her beautiful
picture! Who could have spoiled it in this way?

ANNA. You are the last one that should inquire,
Elsey.

ELSEY. Mary has no friend that can sympathize with
her more deeply than I do. For I am a lover of beautiful pictures. I know a good one and appreciate it.
Mary's was the only one in school better than mine. I
have watched it, and done my best to come up to it,
and have failed.

ANNA. And there was but one way left for you——

MARY. Hush! Anna, hush! "Speak gently!"
"Think kindly!"

ANNA. I despise hypocrites! I can't tolerate their
presence.

ELSEY. Anna Tibbets, you had better turn your
face to the wall. I despise your mean, suspicious eye.
I understand your base insinuations; they reveal the
black heart from which they spring. I will exchange
no word with you.

ANNA. That is well, since my eye is too keen for
you to deceive. Words exchanged with you would be
useless.

ELSEY. Turn your face to the wall—I would not
look upon it.

ANNA. Leave this room, base hypocrite!

ELSEY. I will turn my back upon you while I speak to Mary. Twenty gold medals would I give, if I had them, to restore the beauty of your picture.

ANNA. The thing you have done you can 't undo.

MARY. Anna, why will you? Your hard words mar the beauty of your life. There is more than one picture spoiled this morning. Throw over your shoulders the mantle of charity.

ANNA. The mantle of charity would not become me in this case. Truth should be wielded fearlessly, even if it cuts to the quick.

MARY. Elsey, do not feel disturbed. Innocence will protect itself. I accept your sympathy for the loss of my picture, and congratulate you on the evening's honor.

ELSEY. The medal is yours, Mary Morn; I could not receive it. But let me ask you one question, what do you suppose led Anna Tibbets to daub your picture over in this manner? If she had done the same thing to mine, I would pour molten lead into her eyes. She should never see to daub another.

MARY. O, Anna did n't do it. Nobody did it. Did you read in the paper this morning the account of a fiery serpent writhing himself in our atmosphere?

ELSEY. Yes. What do you think of it?

MARY. I think he spit some of his venom upon my picture, and spoiled it, and there is no use in talking any more about it. The thing is done and can 't be helped.

ELSEY. That may be true, Mary; but he used some

mortal's hand to do his work of deviltry. Now, we will not rest until we find that hand and sever it from the wrist.

ANNA. We might as well cut yours off at once, then, Elsey.

ELSEY. We'll take yours first, Anna: and when the serpent uses mine in that wicked way, I will willingly make the sacrifice.

[*Enter* MRS. HILL *with her little boy.*]

MRS. HILL. Mary, I heard this morning of your spoiled picture. I regret it deeply. Can I do anything to restore its beauty?

MARY. Nothing, Mrs. Hill. It is irreparably gone. A sad disappointment came over me for a moment, but it has passed away.

ELSEY. Nothing remains now to be done but to punish the offender. The hand that spoiled Mary's picture shall be severed from the wrist.

ANNA. Mrs. Hill, have you a sharp knife with you? We might as well proceed at once to the work. I will do the job. I detest hypocrites.

ELSEY. Turn your face to the wall, Anna Tibbets.

MARY. Mrs. Hill, we want no sharp knife, but we all want the beautiful and comfortable "Mantle of Charity."

MRS. HILL. The severe penalty passed upon the offender startles me, for my sweet boy must make the sacrifice. Bennie, darling, go hold up your little hand to Anna.

(*Bennie's little hand is full of flowers. He offers them to Mary. She takes them, kisses the hand, then looks at it — she looks at his white apron all soiled with paint; then unrolls her picture and holds it near him. He kisses it, rubs his hands over it, then wipes it with his apron. Now he looks into Mary's face. Bennie says,* "Me love the pretty baby.")

MARY. (*Kisses him.*) Beautiful innocence! You love my picture! You have loved it to death. Precious hand! Go, throw over Anna's shoulder the mantle of charity.

ANNA. Come, Bennie. I am humbled. I need it.

MRS. HILL. Mary, I am sadly distressed for the loss of your picture. Forgive my carelessness. Last evening I let Bennie come into the hall with Jane to amuse themselves. I did not think he could do any mischief. When he came home he was daubed over with paint. Jane had been interested in her book, and could give no account of where he got it. I tried to wash it from his hand, but he fought me away, saying, "No, no; Bennie love it." So I put my darling to bed with the mark upon him; and here he is now. I commend him to your mercy.

MARY. The darling! I forgive him. His love for my picture is unmistakable. His innocence shields him from guilt. The baby artist! He destroys now, but when the wisdom of years rests upon him, he will create.

MRS. HILL. Bennie, kiss Mary, and say " I 'm sorry."

(*He kisses her, and tries to take the picture from her hand.*)

MARY. Blessed boy! I will paint you a prettier one than this.

MRS. HILL. We must go. Good-bye. [*Exit.*

ELSEY. And I, too, must go. I only came in to sympathize with you in your loss. I have already stayed too long. [*Exit* ELSEY.

ANNA. I have been hasty, Mary; but who would have thought little Bennie Hill did the mischief?

MARY. No one could think it; but we could all withhold censure until we were quite sure of the one that merited it, and even then we should speak it gently. Reproof given in love has a softening influence.

ANNA. Mary, have you heard the report that is flying through the country about Elsey's brother Carl?

MARY. No. What is it?

ANNA. Mr. Churchill has lost five thousand dollars from his office. Carl was the only one in there the day it disappeared. Then you know he started that same night in a great hurry for Kansas. I suppose there is not much doubt but he took it. Circumstances are strongly against him.

MARY. O, Anna, do not be so ready to believe those slanderous reports! Wait for a better proof than circumstances. Always stand on the side of innocence — hope for it; plead for it. Carl loves fun, and sometimes goes too far, but he is not a thief. I will stand by him in this dark hour.

ANNA. And suppose he is guilty?

MARY. If he is guilty he must be punished. I do not believe he is guilty, so we will not talk of punishment.

ANNA. Circumstances are against him, and we may as well look things in the face. Somebody has taken the money.

MARY. Be it so; and let us feel pity,

"For sure it must be a weary lot,
  The sin-stained heart to bear."

[*Enter* CARL.]

CARL. Is Elsey here?

MARY. She was here a moment since.

CARL. Where is she now? Tell me quick. I am in a fearful haste.

MARY. What has happened, Carl?

CARL. Five hundred dollars reward offered for my head. Telegrams are flying all over the country; one met me in Kansas. I did not wait for a stranger to lay hands on me. I flew home. I must see Elsey. The sheriffs are all awake. I have no time to lose. Any moment one of them may be upon me.

MARY. What can Elsey do for you?

CARL. I will yield myself into her hands. She may give me to the sheriff and claim the reward. You know mother is poorer than poverty itself. If I am buried in prison she would suffer. Tell me, where is Elsey?

MARY. I don't know, Carl; but answer me one question, Did you steal the money?

CARL. Give me your hand, Mary. Over this I swear I never touched the money. Your hand, to me, Mary, is as sacred as the Bible. But where shall I find Elsey? If I meet a sheriff on the street the money is lost.

MARY. Can I help you?

CARL. Yes; accept me as your prisoner. Put me somewhere under guard, and then go claim the reward for my mother.

MARY.   I 'll do it, Carl.

ANNA.   I hear the sheriff's heavy tread now; he has got track of you.

MARY.   Run, Carl, into this side room.

[*Enter* SHERIFF.]

SHERIFF.   Miss Morn, is Elsey Green here?

MARY.   She was here a few minutes ago, but is not now.

SHERIFF.   I suppose she knows where her brother is?

MARY.   She did not speak of him.   I do not think she knows there is any charge against him.   I am sorry suspicion has fallen upon poor Carl.   I believe he is innocent.   The family are very poor.   They cannot well afford to have him pay the penalty of the guilty.

SHERIFF.   I have considered the poverty of the family.   I know them well.   Mrs. Green is in poor health.   I thought if Elsey knew her brother's whereabouts, she might be induced to tell me and secure the reward for her mother.

MARY.   Do you think Elsey would betray her brother for five hundred dollars?

SHERIFF.   Some one will; and I feel pity for the family, and would like to manage the matter so that they might have the reward.

MARY.   But Carl did n't take the money.

SHERIFF.   That is n't my business.   I am to find him.

MARY.   Sheriff, I know his hiding place.   If I reveal it to you, will you trust the five hundred dollars in my hand for his mother?

SHERIFF.   I will.

MARY.   I have your promise; and here is Anna, she will be witness to the agreement.

SHERIFF. I accept Anna as witness. (*Takes a paper and pencil from his pocket.*) Please write his present address on this card.

(*Mary writes and gives to the Sheriff.*)

SHERIFF (*reads*). " In the side room of the house we now occupy." What does this mean, Miss Morn?

MARY. It means he is here. Shall I bring him forward? But is the reward sure?

SHERIFF. Bring him forward, and the reward is sure!

(*Mary opens the door. Carl walks in.*)

SHERIFF. What does this mean? Have you not been in Kansas?

CARL. Yes; and I met one of the flying telegrams there, and hastened home to respond in person to the friendly call. I am at your service, Sheriff.

SHERIFF. All right. You are the boy we want. The law must have its course; and we'll hope to prove you innocent.

CARL. I will trust for that. I had a dream last night. I saw Mr. Churchill's money crowded down into the back side of his drawer. I believe it is there now.

MARY. I believe so too. Sheriff, please leave Carl in my keeping while you make the search.

SHERIFF. That will not do. I would trust you, but the law is between us.

[*Enter* ELSEY.]

ELSEY. O, brother Carl! you here? What sent you home?

CARL. I came to secure five hundred dollars to you

and mother. I 've accomplished my object. The money is pledged to Mary. I have had the honor of being her prisoner. She has delivered me into the sheriff's hands.

ELSEY. O, Mary!

MARY. He compelled me to it. But he is innocent, Elsey, and your poor mother will have the five hundred dollars. I know he is innocent.

ELSEY. Of course he is innocent — my brother is innocent; and Mary Morn, with her mantle of charity on, can see it. What does cloudy Anna think?

ANNA. Forgive me, Elsey, I will hope for the best.

ELSEY. The mantle of hope is a little in advance of the serpentine one you had on an hour ago.

SHERIFF. (*Places his hand on Carl's shoulder.*) Come, my boy, I have no time to lose.

ELSEY. Hands off, Mr. Sheriff. My innocent brother does not walk one step with you. (*Takes from her pocket a paper and reads.*)

" MRS. GREEN: I am happy to inform you the lost money is found. I regret the hasty step I have taken, and will try to make proper amends to you and your boy. I found the money crowded tightly into the back side of my drawer. — E. CHURCHILL."

Now, Mr. Sheriff, with all due respect to your office, we discharge you.

SHERIFF. My business is not settled yet. I am bound to Miss Mary for five hundred dollars, which I now pay her. I want a receipt for it. Master Carl must accompany me to Mr. Churchill's office and receive an apology from him. I will put no handcuffs on him. Come along. [*Exeunt* SHERIFF *and* CARL.

ELSEY. The fiery serpent has twice coiled himself

about our humble home to-day, but some good power has foiled his purpose.

MARY. You know it is written in the Book of Books, "He shall give His angels charge over thee, to keep thee." Let us ever trust that promise.

ELSEY. Mary, I have a little trust. We sometimes see ourselves so wonderfully protected — yes, many times; but, on the whole, life is dark and cold.

MARY. Wrap about you " The Mantle of Charity," and you will find it very warm.   [*Curtain falls.*

A PICNIC.

Characters:

SARAH EARL,   AGNES LANE,   ROSIE BRIGHT,
GRACIE DOW,   SUSAN DARLING,   HARRY DAY,
SIDNEY FIELD and FRANK SIMPSON.

All present but GRACIE. SARAH EARL sits at the table, as the presiding genius of the evening, with a pencil in her hand and a sheet of paper on the table. Her head and one shoulder are wreathed in flowers. Her guests are standing with hats on.

SARAH (*rising*). My friends, I am delighted to see you this evening. My heart beats warmly in anticipation of our picnic feast. I am a little impatient at Gracie's tardiness. Shall we begin to unpack our baskets, or shall we wait for her?

MANY VOICES. Wait.

AGNES. She will bring us something worth the waiting. Gracie is always tardy on all occasions when she is particularly wanted; but, when she comes, we find her ready.

HARRY. Yes, Gracie will be fresh. She always puts spice into her dishes.

[*Enter GRACIE in haste, swinging her hat by the string.*]

26

GRACIE. Excuse me; I am sorry to have kept you waiting.

SARAH. We will hear your apology.

GRACIE. Is there no excusing me without it?

MANY VOICES. None — none.

GRACIE. Then, the truth I will tell you, though I speak it with shame. I have a place for everything, but everything isn't in its place; and when I wanted to start for this golden picnic, my gloves were nowhere — and this means, nowhere that I could find them. So I took Lottie's mittens, as you see. (*Holding up her hands.*) Then our pet dog, Carlo, had treated himself to a frolic with my new knit overshoes, which I had left lying in the corner, so I had to wait to warm my rubbers. Then I coasted on the way only half a minute.

SARAH. The beautiful garb of truth is the only salient point in your apology. Our judgment will not be tempered with much mercy in your case. You would not like to be called dishonest, and I am sure there is not much honesty in robbing your friends of some of the precious moments that make up life. As a penalty for your fault, we call upon you for the first dish, and that must be an impromptu poem.

GRACIE. Queen of the Feast! you are very severe. Poor *me* give an impromptu poem! And simply because I robbed you of a few moments of time. I appeal to your people. Let your Queen revoke her command.

ALL. Never — never! Her word is law.

SARAH. Miss Gracie will please bring her dish round to the center of the circle, that each guest may receive a generous share.   Here, take my place.   (*Sarah steps aside to make room for her.   Gracie takes her place.*)

GRACIE.   Our Queen has complimented me very slightly, once this evening, on speaking truth.   Being most desirous for her continued approbation, the truth again I will speak, although the doing it draws severely on my very sensitive nerves.   You will appreciate, I trust, the effort it costs me, since it is but the laying my dear self upon the altar for sacrifice :

> " We have no right to others' time,
>   Our promise we should keep ;
>   Thus, pardon me, good friends and kind —
>   Pardon — or I must weep.
>
> " Some little minutes you have lost,
>   While I my gloves did seek ;
>   Then Carlo took my shoes in sport,
>   And spoiled them in his freak.
>
> " So rubbers I must wait to warm,
>   And minutes flew away ;
>   Then coasting offered such a charm,
>   I yielded to its sway.
>
> " But we 've no right to others' time,
>   Our promise we should keep ;
>   Please pardon me, good friends and kind,
>   Pardon — or I must weep."

(All greatly applaud.)

SARAH.   Pardon is granted.   You have generously canceled your obligation to us.   Now, whose basket shall we peep into next?

HARRY.   I wish it might be mine.   You all know I am but " poor scholar," and sweep the school-room to pay my tuition bill. My brain is as poor as my purse. The teacher says, there is only one bump on it that will pay for a college life; so you see my choice of viands for this picnic has been limited, and the dry bone I bring you to pick, should be presented while the appetite is keen from fasting. Do not infer from these remarks that I undervalue Gracie's savory dish. On the contrary, 't is that which urges me to present mine at an early hour.

FRANK, *the Farmer.* I have no petition to make to our kind hostess, but would simply suggest to her good sense, the propriety of a farmer's dish next.

SARAH. The farmer's dish we will receive, hoping it will strengthen the ultimates of life, so that we may be able, later in the evening, to digest the wisdom of our modest student.

HARRY. I must abide the decision of our Queen. Since she has denied my first wish, let me speak a second one: let my offering be the dessert — *a nut to crack.*

SARAH. Very appropriate there. Will our Farmer take his place here? (*He changes places with Gracie.*)

(FARMER *places upon the table a wing.*)

(*All smile.*)

AGNES. We expected you would bring us some cabbage and potatoes.

GRACIE. No; we expected a drove of pigs driven in here. I heard them squeal a moment ago.

FARMER. Well, I have disappointed you both. A farmer has to take everything in its season. He can 't make hay in December, nor drive pigs to market in the evening. What is in my mind *to-day* I have brought you. A farmer raises poultry, as well as pigs. I had some hundred of the Shanghai hens — not to name the crowers — and every morning, when I went to give them their breakfast, I would find some of them missing. I suspected a thief had found an entrance into my yard, so I set a trap for him in the evening. In the early morning a large cat owl, caught by one leg, was making strenuous exertions to gain her liberty. I rushed forward exultantly, exclaiming, "Rogue! Thief! I have you at last." Poor owl seated herself in the quietude of despair, then fixed her great, round eyes upon me reproachfully, and said, "'T is true, you have me at last. I am your captive. But don't be in haste to finish your work of destruction —

> "But listen to me — for hear me ye must —
> An innocent owl ye have laid in the dust;
> Thy ruthless hand hath determined my fate,
> And plunged in despair my desolate mate.

> "To ease your conscience, sir farmer, do ye say,
> Thrice on your hens I ventured to prey?
> The charge I admit — to the deed I had right,
> For nature hath formed me to plunder by night.

> "Ah, here is the rub — for the sake of poached egg,
> You contrived to catch poor owl by the leg;
> But the deed is done, so me ye may roast,
> And, in the meantime, I will drink you a toast:

> "Here is hoping my mate will eat, by fourscore,
> The very best hens that feed by your door;
> Here is hoping again, your hens will ne'er lay —
> Never more may you find a nest in the hay."

This speech of my captive, with her fright and the great exertions she had made to gain her liberty, was too much. Poor owl tumbled upon her back, and when I cut the cord that bound her, she was no more — I held in my hand a lifeless form, covered with feathers. Her wing I bring, as an offering, to the picnic.

AGNES. 'T was too bad to kill such a sensible owl. What a sense of justice she showed!

GRACIE. She showed a vindictive spirit. What a severe toast she drank for your benefit, Frank. I do not think she was prepared to die. You should have given her time for repentance.

FRANK. She was too quick for me. I had cut her prison-cord, and was just going to whistle the air of "Liberty," when she fell into so sound a sleep I could not wake her. She hurried off. I do not think she had it in her heart to forgive me.

SUSIE. And she could not, Frank. Poor owl was never born into the light of forgiveness. She was true to her instinct. Let us be as true to our reason. Catty owl had large, leaden eyes; she could not raise them to heaven, and learn the angelic lesson of overcoming evil with good. Such wisdom is in reserve for us. We have eyes of light that can traverse the world of mind.

ROSIE. O, yes, Susie; and we know right from wrong — good from evil. And we can see the true and the beautiful. Look at these flowers! (*Holds up her bouquet.*)

SARAH. We are greatly indebted to our farmer friend. And now, if our traveler from the north will raise the lid of his basket, we are prepared for another treat. Mr. Field, will he walk this way?

(MR. FIELD *lays upon the table a very small phial of water.*)

GRACIE. O, Mr. Field, you have brought us a bottle of Homœopathic medicine. Who did you think was sick?

MR. FIELD. I did not think any one was sick. We were all to bring something of that which interested us most, as our farmer said, *to-day*. So I have brought you some water from the Falls of Niagara.

ROSIE. O, traveler, did n't you break the Falls in bringing such a bountiful fountain to our picnic?

MR. FIELD. Do n't ridicule me, flower girl, till you have knelt in reverence at the base of God's great waters. This little phial holds all that I could bring away; but the mighty whole is there. It was there — it is there — it will be there forever. We, puny children, come and go; the great Falls, never. In their diamond light, their rainbow circle, their perpetual motion, we see the image of Him who holds their power in the hollow of His hand; and who is the same to-day, yesterday, and forever.

ROSIE. But, Mr. Field, you should have written a poem there, for our picnic. Everybody that goes to the Niagara Falls must write a poem. I have mine half written now.

MR. FIELD. Well, I advise you to burn it up, to save yourself the blush that will mantle your cheek when you stand before the great reality. But, I have my poem. The very small phial of water I brought away is typical of it:

> " Thousands have come, beheld, and gone,
>   With admiration drank their fill,
> And thousands, thousands yet unborn,
>   Shall feast their souls upon thee still."

MANY VOICES. You have done well, Mr. Traveler.

SUSIE. 'Tis a little too condensed, but we accept it with gratitude.

SARAH. Will our thinker, Miss Bright, give us her dish?

(SUSAN *takes the center, and lays a dry leaf upon the table.*)

HARRY. That dry leaf looks rather dry. My hard, dry nut might with propriety follow it.

SUSAN. Our modest "poor scholar" may see that there is a lesson of wisdom to be drawn from a dry leaf. Early in the autumn, when the bright red and the beautiful yellow leaves were fast falling to the ground, a sadness stole over my spirit, and I broke from our cherry tree this dry, withering branch. Then I felt a presence near me, and these words fell softly upon my ear:

> " Though leaves are falling, falling, falling everywhere,
>   All the sweetest blooms of spring,
>   That open when the robins sing,
>   Are on the apple, plum, and pear,
>   And the cherry pure and fair,
>   They are all close to the branches bare.
>   Just see the smoothly-rounded forms,
>   Safely shielded from all storms
>   In these glossy, bright, brown buds."

Here I ceased to listen, and fixed my eye intently on the wonderful bud, in which lies, deeply and mysteriously concealed, the luscious fruit. And I saw in the little brown buds,

> " Prophecies of gentle days,
>   Of violet-beds and wild-bird lays."

Then, though the leaves have fallen, fallen everywhere,

> " And the wind is chill and cold,
> And the snow lies on the ground,
> And the year is growing old,
> And the fields are bare,"

do they not tell us, in sweetest tones, that spring's fair
days will come again?

> " Days of bloom — warm days of light,
> Sunny skies and waters bright,
> Singing brooks and gentle showers,
> Mossy banks and smiling flowers;
> Yes, all the budding branches sing,
> Winter leads to smiling spring."

ROSIE.   O, Miss Bright, your dry branch has opened
to us worlds of hidden wisdom. Who could have thought
so much of life and beauty was concealed in those dry
buds!

SARAH.   Yes; we are very much indebted to Miss
Bright for distilling such an odorous extract from a dry
branch. Will Agnes, our singing nursery girl, open
her basket for us next?

AGNES.   With much pleasure. (*She lays a doll on
the table.*)   I knew you would all laugh at my offering.
This doll is only a waxen representative of the living
beauties of which I shall speak:

> ' Is there aught more fair than flowers
>   Blooming in the light of May?
> Than the birdlings in the bowers,
>   Singing all their lives away?

> " Is there aught that beams more brightly,
>   Than the sunlight on the sea?
> Is there aught that skips more lightly
>   Than the lambkin o'er the lea?"

Yes, I know what is fairer and brighter than even beautiful flowers and golden sunbeams; and I know what skips more lightly in their innocence than lambkin's o'er the lea:

> " Little babies — they were given
>   By the Father of us all,
> As a link 'twixt earth and heaven,
>   After man's unhappy fall.

> " Dimpled cheeks and rosy faces,
>   Silken hair and laughing eyes —
> These are nature's finest traces,
>   Here her greatest beauty lies.

> " Little babies ! Father, bless them,
>   Keep them safe from every harm ;
> Holy angels, kindly press them
>   To your bosoms, soft and warm."

Well, I bring to the picnic the babies — the brightest link between earth and heaven.

SARAH. The babies are very welcome to our feast. It would not be full without them. Now we are ready for our flower girl. Will Miss Rosie walk this way?

ROSIE. (*Places on the table a bouquet.*) My offering unlike the others, needs no human voice to speak for it. 'T is itself a beautiful poem. It has been said by some one, that music is the voice of God, and poetry — His language. I offer these flowers as the perfect embodiment of both.

SARAH. Thank you, Rosie, we accept your fragrant poem. Now we are ready for the dessert. Will our modest " poor scholar " bring in his dish of nuts ?

HARRY. I think we have had a sumptuous entertainment this evening. We are all satisfied. We crave no more. Then, ladies and gentlemen, if you will withdraw, I will sweep, dust the room, and put things to rights here.

SARAH. Not at all. Are we satisfied without our dessert?

MANY VOICES. Come this way.

HARRY. In the presence of all the luxurious wealth displayed here this evening, I feel myself more than usually pinched with poverty. I have but one gift. The gift of numbers is too dry for a social picnic. When I was a very little child, and I sat upon my mother's knee, she taught me to say,

> " Twice one are two, twice two are four,
>   And six are three times two :
>   Twice four are eight, twice five are ten —"

And more than this I can't do, so please excuse me. (*He starts to leave.*)

MANY VOICES. No, no; come back — come back.

HARRY. (*Lays a dead mouse upon the table. A general laugh and applause.*) Mathematics are abstract numbers — dry bones — hard nuts to crack. 'T was not an easy task, to find a suitable representative of what I wish to say, to lay upon your table beside the flowers and babies. (*Takes his mouse and places it close to the flowers, and then lays the doll the other side of it.*) You see this mouse, 't is a representative of a live animal of the same species. You have read in natural history that another species of animals, called cats, have a strong partiality for these little defenceless creatures that we call mice, and they often lie in ambush for them in a sly manner and catch them. Now the nut I give you to crack is this: Supposing three wicked cats could catch three defenceless mice in three days, how many days would it take a hundred cats to catch a hundred mice?

GRACIE. A hundred days.

HARRY. You are cloyed with the rich variety of dishes you have had this evening. I knew you could not digest mine.

MANY VOICES. One hundred days, of course.

HARRY. You are wrong. I appeal to the presiding genius of the evening.

SARAH. (*Takes pencil and paper a moment.*) If it takes three cats three days to catch three mice, it must take one cat three days to catch one mouse; therefore, it must take a hundred wicked cats three hundred days to catch one hundred defenceless mice. Am I right?

HARRY. You certainly are, and your manner of cracking the nut must satisfactorily prove it to all. Now, may I be excused? I've done my best.

SARAH. You are excused. Accept our thanks. The first day of next month, I shall hope to see you all here again, bringing any friend with you that may like to come.

HARRY. Let "poor scholar" sweep the room to pay his tuition. [*Curtain falls.*

CANDY-PULLING.

Characters:

GRANTVILLE AMES,
HETTIE, *his Sister*,
MYRTLE LANE,
KATE NORTH,

HANNAH HUGH,
JOSHUA EARLE,
FORDYCE DEWEY,
CAPT. ORSON.

GRANTVILLE AMES alone, walking the stage in an angry mood and excited manner.

[*Enter his Sister.*]

HETTIE. Grant., I am glad to find you here. We want you in the dining-room. We have a gay party there.

GRANT. Go, and enjoy it, then, sister, and not come here to invite a thunderbolt into your midst.

HETTIE. But, we want you to enjoy it with us.

GRANT. Not a bit of it. I've no heart for sunshine this evening.

HETTIE. What's the matter, Grantie? You look like night in the Polar regions.

GRANT. Gentle sister, leave me. Go, enjoy your gay friends. Do you hear the angry howling of contending winds outside?

HETTIE. No. I've no ear for the angry voice of the

38

winds. I hear only sweet melodies. Come, join us, and we will put your harp in good tune.

GRANT. Touch not my harp. 'T is tuned by furies. I will fight them alone. Leave me, sister; seek the the sunshine.

HETTIE. I must leave you, Grant., for the girls will wonder at my delay; but I wish you would join us. We are having a great candy - pulling, and we want your assistance.

GRANT. I am having a candy - pulling too; but I must pull it alone.

HETTIE. Let me help you.

GRANT. You cannot. Your ear is tuned only to harmony. Away — away!

HETTIE. I go, then, but unwillingly. [*Exit.*

GRANT. (*Takes a letter from the table and reads.*)

" Our wise scheme for sudden riches has proved a bubble. The company burst the day after we joined it. What money we invested, the devil has swallowed. All is gone."

Well, Dan. uses strong language; and I'm in a mood for it. I have listened to many lessons on the Divine Providence; but I doubt if there be such a thing. Chance is king of the day and king of the night, and the whimsical old fellow is beyond the reach of the keenest intellect. Two men start on a journey together, one is safely led to a mine of gold; the other, full of ideas and high aspirations, is left to struggle with grim want. I believe nothing, only this: Every man has got candy to pull, and he finds it hard work, for he is as likely to pull the wrong way as the right.

[*Enter* HETTIE, *pulling candy.*]

HETTIE. Come, brother Grantie; you don't know how much we do want you to help us. We have got lots of candy, and 't is hard to pull.

GRANT. Day and night, summer and winter, play and work,—we have all got candy to pull. Sister, doesn't the pulling of so much candy distract your mind?

HETTIE. It tires my arm, and I want you to help us.

GRANT. Do not mind a little arm-ache. I would relish that, if the head was clear and the heart at ease.

HETTIE. Join our party, and it will lighten your head and rest your heart. Myrtie Lane has just come in. Now, you cannot resist her attractions. She is in one of her plaintive moods, and needs your presence to make her eyes sparkle.

GRANT. Myrtie Lane! Do not mention her name to *me*. Why is she in *our* home? What tempted her *here?*

HETTIE. And should not Myrtie Lane visit our home? She has been the mutual friend of our school-days. She has followed you with interest through all your college life; and, now, you say, "What tempted her *here?*"

GRANT. Yes, I say it; she ought not to be here. But Myrtie cannot err; she has a reason, and Grantville Ames, in this tumult of feeling, cannot perceive it. Has she inquired for me?

HETTIE. No. She came over to bring some medicine to ma.

GRANT. I knew she had a reason for coming. Now, hurry back, or she will be gone.

HETTIE. 'T is too bad that you will not help us pull our candy. *[Exit.*

GRANT. Pulling candy is *play* for the girls. Well, I'm glad my good sister does n't know the bitter candy I am pulling. She speaks lightly to me of Myrtle Lane; says she is in our home. Her words came near stifling me. The heart gave one bound, and then paused. An angel is in my home. I know it. Sister tells me so. But — well, I am shut out. Chance rules the day — a most unjust and wayward ruler. I would blast the demon from existence. He has given me no fortune, no fame, no position in life. Were this all the wrong he has done me, I could bear it. But, in every attempt I make to rise, he pulls from underneath me the stepping-stone, then grins at my discomfiture. Even this I might bear; but his last satanic push is the drop too much. Curse him, all ye powers of earth! Curse him, all ye powers of hell!

[*Enter* CAPT. ORSON.]

CAPT. O. Hold, my good friend! 'T is well ye do not call on heaven for a curse. (*Takes him warmly by the hand.*) What has happened to you? On whom are you invoking this curse?

GRANT. The demon, Chance. He is ruler of earth, if not of heaven, and I curse his black name.

CAPT. O. My young friend, Grantville Ames, come out of this fearful darkness. Seek again the light of Providence. Hold on to your father's blessed faith.

GRANT. My father's faith! 'T was buried in the grave with his body. The remembrance of it only makes darkness the more blinding. My father had light to guide him; his son is the victim of a cruel despot. I writhe in these iron chains. I will burst them or die.

CAPT. O. Grant., be calm. Quiet your ruffled feathers.

GRANT. I can't do it, Capt. Orson.

> "There are times when in the heart
> The storm of feeling rises high;
> And thoughts, like forked lightnings, dart
> Athwart the spirit's gloomy sky.
> When, passion wildly o'er the soul,
> Holds high its power with demon pride,
> And wisdom's voice has no control
> To calm or check the swelling tide.
> When all that's holy, good, and bright,
> And all that's beautiful and fair,
> Within the spirit's world of light,
> Lies wrecked in wild confusion there."

(*He sinks into a chair, and rests his head on his hand.*)

CAPT. O. My poor boy! you are in troubled waters, and your faith is weak. Do you remember when Peter found himself sinking, he cried, " Lord, save me, or I perish."

GRANT. I do remember; but I've no voice now. Friend of my father, cry it for me.

CAPT. O. The Lord doth not wait for the voice. He saw thee sinking, and has sent me to bid thee be of good courage. This evening, in my room, I was reading His Word, to prepare myself for a child's sleep, when suddenly I was brought to a pause. I could not continue, so I went back and read, " He shall give His angels charge over thee, to bear thee up in their hands, lest thou dash thy foot against a stone." Again I paused;

I could read no more. My book was closed, coat and hat put on, and I found myself out in the pitiless snow storm. No chance brought me here. Speak, boy. I have weathered many a storm at sea, and I can help thee right thy sinking ship.

GRANT. Capt. Orson, your kindness has stilled the soul's tempest. I feel a calm, but no voice to speak

CAPT. O. Grantville, I have traveled a long journey. You see my frosty hair tells of many winters; and if you examine it closely, you will see a silvery warmth there, that tells of many summers too. I have had my youth, and it hath not passed from me; it lives still, and would enter into all your sympathies. If money matters trouble you, my bank is at your service. If the heart bleeds,—be patient, boy. You see your old friend, a bachelor of seventy summers; he was young once—he can never forget. But, speak child; I am here for it.

GRANT. Shall I speak all? May I be a child? And will you keep me safe?

CAPT. O. Speak all; be a child. Let me stand in your father's place. There is a void in my withering heart that the freshness of your life may fill.

GRANT. 'T is nearly a year since father died, and left me in charge of mother and Hettie, with only a small competency. I was impatient to increase it. I dreamed of sudden wealth, and was fool enough to invest all the money I could command in a miasmatic bubble which has burst, and its noxious effluvia is almost suffocating to us, silly fools, that inflated it. I had just learned of this, when a dispatch came, informing me of the loss of a vessel that father had sent to the West Indies, and no insurance. These two losses were nearly our all, and I groaned over them, but still kept up strong, hoping that I could take care of mother and sister by my own exertions. I had already applied for a professorship in B—— university, and was sanguine of gaining it. While I held the first two missiles in my hand, a third came : I was too young for the professorship I sought. And here you find me, captain.

CAPT. O. Well, I can right this ship easily. But, is this all? Could a little matter of money so quake the earth under your feet, as to make you reel like a young sailor at sea? Be honest, Grantville. I am your confessor. Make a clear conscience.

GRANT. 'Tis not all. 'Twas the last bitter drop that unnerved me; and it came so unmerited, so uncalled-for. (*Takes a letter from his pocket, and crushes it between his hands.*) Mean, cowardly offspring of a mean, miserly mind! Blast the deathly thing! (*He thrusts, angrily, the letter into his pocket again.*)

CAPT. O. Grantville, let me examine the sharp sword that has pierced you?

GRANT. 'Tis long, 'twould weary your life; 'tis dirty, 'twould soil your hands. In few words I can give you the edge of it. You know the loveliest girl in Kedron. I need not name her. Our birthdays are the same; I am one year her senior. I remember, when only two years old, rocking the pretty baby in her cradle. When her mother came to take her up, I fought her away like a hero. I said, " Pretty baby is all mine." This saying brought the house down with laughter, and merry jokes were passed between the mothers, which I did not fully comprehend then, but I understand them now. The pretty baby nestled herself cosily into the inmost of my heart; I have ever held her there in worshiping love. She is my inner and better self; and when this withering letter came from her father, wrenching her from my life, with the one word " *Never*," it made me what you found me — a fury- a madman — raving and wild.

CAPT. O. We will try and right this matter too. I sympathize with you. I know it all — I feel it all. Years has not blunted the heart's sensibilities. I had a Myrtle once. She was my soul's life, and she is my soul's life now; she was taken from me, and yet I hold her. I only name this that you may understand that I am a living man, and feel for you. Now to your angel; is she at home in the cosy nest you have made so warm for her?

GRANT. I know she is, and yet I have never questioned her. We have never talked of love; the feeling has satisfied us.

CAPT. O. You say *we*, and speak confidently.

GRANT. I speak what I know, and my knowledge is deeper and surer than words could make it. Do I not know that Myrtle Lane is all mine — was mine in her cradle? Her cruel father has come between us with the " *Never*." Divide a heart, and the lungs soon cease their play. Dr. Lane may do with his surgical knife more than he intends.

CAPT. O. What objections has the Dr. to your suit?

GRANT. I did n't know that he had any, until I received his letter. It seems Joshua Earle, who has recently come into possession of two fortunes, has sought his daughter's hand. The old man is dazzled with the splendor of his wealth, and fearing lest I might stand in Earle's way, he wrote me this very impudent letter, evidently intending to make me angry, accusing me of tricks that are as far from my nature as the North Pole is from the South. He finished his abuse by taunting me with poverty, and commanding me not only never to cross the threshold of his door again, but *never* to speak to his daughter, should I chance to meet her.

CAPT. O. Do you intend to obey his commands?

GRANT. I will never cross the threshold of his door again, unless he is outside of it.

CAPT. O. Are you sure of this, boy?

GRANT. I would walk over his head to see his daughter.

CAPT. O. Keep cool, Grantville. Your "pretty baby" is my pet. The blood of my Myrtle is in her veins, and her silly father shall never sacrifice her happiness on the shrine of Mammon, rest in this assurance. I have power, and will see to it. Now, one word of money matters. Enter into no more speculations. Whatever money you want, draw upon my bank; there is a surplus there, and I am glad to find an outlet for it. What are your plans?

GRANT. I would like to travel a year, and then enter upon my profession.

CAPT. O. That is good. Travel a year, or more, as you think it may be of use to you. I would visit all the eminent hospitals. Fit yourself to stand strong on the topmost round of the ladder of surgery. Your profession is a good one. Your mother and sister shall be cared for in your absence. And pretty Myrtle's hand I will guard. It shall not be given without the heart is in it. I would sooner have it cut from her wrist. Call on me in the morning, and we will have things all arranged.

GRANT. Captain Orson, I've no words —

CAPT. O. That's good; words are not needed now. Good night. [*Exit.*

GRANT. How suddenly has the brightest day dawned upon the darkest night! Only one hour ago, I was a boiling cauldron of doubt, fear, dread, and hate; now a happy child of faith, trust, hope, and love.

[*Enter* HETTIE, *with candy in her hand.*]

HETTIE. Grantie, our candy is all pulled. Will you have a piece?

GRANT. Thank you, dear sister; I could not eat of yours. Mine is all pulled too; some day I shall treat you to a piece of it, but not now; age will improve it.

HETTIE. I am glad you have got your candy pulled straight, for you look happy now. Why did n't you let me help you?

GRANT. Your soft hands are too delicate; but I had help. I could never have done it alone. How long did Myrtle stay with you?

HETTIE. She was gone when I got back. She was in great haste. She only came to bring ma some medicine. But will you not come with me now?

GRANT. Yes; I am already to keep you good company. [*Exeunt.*

SCENE SECOND.

Joshua Earle walking the stage, with hands behind him, and a half-satisfied air.

JOSHUA.

"This world is all a fleeting show,
For man's illusion given."

So says the poet, and I believe he speaks truly. I doubt if there is any reality in life. All the world envies me, and yet I am restless. A fortune has just rained into my hands, and what is it? I feel nothing; and yet it has brought about me a wonderful change. I am now surrounded with a host of admiring friends. Sometimes they tire me. I have a large mansion of a house, all elegantly furnished; but it's dreadful lonely there. Young ladies, with their managing ma's, call on me; they bring me flowers, and, I suppose, they expect I shall sigh over them; but I leave them to wither on the table. And they bring me honeyed words too. I understand them; they want to take possession of my hive. What a world of honey-bees flit about me! I am not a fool; I know some of them would sting me, if they caught me. There is only one sweet bee that I could tolerate here, and she flits from me. Her ambitious papa says "Yes," in his blandest manner, and I know why; but she, fairy, angel, or whatever you may call her, is not caught by gilded trappings.

[*Enter* FORDYCE DEWEY.]

FOR. I have come, my good old friend, to congratulate you. There is no end to the blessings a fortune brings. And while I congratulate you, I have to condole with many of the fair sex, who had indulged a hope.

JOSH. My fortune does n't add to my happiness. I may get used to it by-and-by. When I was a salesman in Derby's store, I had a purpose in life. Friends were few then, but real; and life was earnest and active. I took hold of things, and they seemed substantial.

FOR. I should think you had enough now to feel some substance. Your fortune has gained you the prettiest girl in Kedron. Is not she substantial?

JOSH. The least of all; I cannot reach her. She is too etherial for my coarse hand. To be sure, her father has given her to me; but what of that? She is n't mine. She is n't one of those honey-bees that seeks a fine hive. But I like her mighty well; her shyness pleases me. When I try to say nice things to her, I get confused, she changes so fast; sometimes her cheeks are like red roses, and I take courage; sometimes she turns white like a winding-sheet, then, man as I am, I tremble.

FOR. Why do n't you marry her at once, if you have the old man's consent?

JOSH. When I named it to her, all the color left her cheeks. I saw her shiver; one tear fell; then she whispered, "Not yet; you and pa have made the bargain; you must wait a while for me. I do n't know myself. I must try to do as pa wishes me to." Something like this she said, and I tell you my face was n't very white. I felt the blood keep rising under my hair. I guess we did n't either feel very easy in ourselves.

She did n't move at all.   I hitched round a good deal, trying to find some words to say back to her; but when I found I was choking, I gathered my boots together, and said, "Good night, Miss Lane."   I have n't seen her since.

FOR.   You are a fool, Josh. Earle, with all your money.   If I were in your place, and wanted the girl, I would marry her before the next new moon.

JOSH.   And I think you would have a sorrowful honey-moon.   No, Ford., I will not marry that pretty girl against her will.   I would n't mind taking her against her father's will, if she liked me.   The liking is what makes the marrying.   I will wait for her awhile, then gather up my boots once more, and listen to her gentle whisper.   I like her mighty well; and this liking does me good; it 's a kind of feeling I encourage.

FOR.   I should think it was rather dangerous business for you.   You may find this feeling troublesome, if your fluttering bird continues to say, " wait."

JOSH.   But it is a good feeling, Ford.; it is the only hope I have in life.   The fortune that has rained so unexpectedly into my pocket does n't amount to anything.   I was Josh. Earle before I had it, and I am Josh. Earle now.   Some people call me *Esquire* Earle; but that calling amounts to just nothing.   This feeling that I was speaking of is something — it 's part of myself — and, as I said, I like to cherish it.

FOR.   What will become of this feeling if Miss Lane should never like you?

JOSH.   I am prepared for that emergency, and I do n't much expect she ever will like me; but, as I said,

I like her mighty well — well enough to marry her. Yet it takes two likings to make a real marriage, and I detest shams — more especially since I have had a glimpse of fashionable life. Ford., I tell you the world is heartless, and them honey-bees that buzz round a handsome hive are the most heartless of all.

FOR. In the beginning of this sensible speech, you said you were prepared for an emergency. I am interested to know in what way, for the knowledge may prove of use to your poor friend sometime, who does not stand much chance of ever being blessed with the two likings you speak of.

JOSH. Well, this is it: There is Betsey Lee — you 've never seen her, Ford. Now, I know in our early days, when we both went barefoot, and ate dry bread for our supper, and a cold potato for our breakfast, she had a liking for me, and I had a liking for her, too. We drank water out of the same bucket, at the old well. She called me Josh., and I called her Bets.; and we always looked after each other's comfort. When I broke my leg trying to ride her grand'ther's old cow, she came in and read Æsop's Fables to me. Them was substantial times, Ford.

FORD. This country Betsey of yours would n't know how to manage a splendid mansion, Josh.

JOSH. Neither do I; but we would manage it in our own way. Betsey has got a feeble ma, that would grow strong in that large, airy south room. Then her blind grand'ther could take the room back of it; this one is n't very pleasant, but, as long as he is blind, 't would n't make any difference to him. Her two brothers could have one of the upper rooms. Then we'd find a nice room for her Aunt Sally. You see, Ford., if I get all them folks into my house, 't would begin to seem like a home; and 't would make them so comfortable too.

For. Well, Josh., you are becoming a philanthropist. Is n't there a room in your house somewhere for me? I am poor.

Josh. If I get Betsey there, we will fit up one expressly for you. Now, I am beginning to get hold of something. Life seems coming back; and I should n't wonder if Betsey was better for me than that pretty bird I have been trying to catch. She is too much like a sunbeam. Sometimes her light dazzles you; and then, without knowing why, you feel a blindness coming over you. The last time I was there, I began choking. She always calls me Mr. Earle; and she bows very genteelly to me. Now, if I should go to see Betsey, she would grab my hand between both of hers, and exclaim, "Josh., I am so glad to see you." Well, if I was clear of this last affair, I would start to-morrow night for Betsey's home; 't is only two days' ride from here. Would n't she be glad to see me, though?

For. You need n't travel so far as that to find a girl that's glad to see you.

Josh. Fie on all the girls here! There is n't one of them cares a fig for Josh. Earle; 't is his hive they want. There is two of them follow me everywhere I go. I'll be blinded if I can guess how they track me. Ever you hear of gals scenting a fellow in a dog way?

For. I think some of them scent you since you had your fortune?

JOSH. That they do. They bore me to death with their ma's bouquets. I'll never accept another one from any of them. I'm for Betsey now; there's two likings there, and a marriage, may be. Farewell, my pretty, trembling bird. You can't like me; 't is n't your fault. I'm rather coarse — just right for Betsey. Ford., what color paper do they write notes on to genteel ladies?

FOR. Pink, to be sure.

JOSH. I'll write Miss Lane a note this evening. I can never put courage enough into my boots again to speak to her. Then to-morrow I am off for Betsey; won't she be glad to see me? and the old folks too? I tell you, Ford., my hand will be squeezed enough down there in Tarrytown. We'll fix up a room for you — Bets. and I will.

FOR. Josh., how is the feeling now that you like to cherish?

JOSH. 'T is as warm as the sun itself. Now, Ford., let me caution you in this matter. If you have a real, live, true feeling in your heart, cherish it. 'T is a God gift, and better than all the fortunes in creation.

[*Enter* KATE NORTH *and* HANNAH HUGH.]

HANNAH. Esquire Earle, ma sent you a bunch of her preserved grapes, with her compliments, and would deem it an honor if you would spend the evening with us. We are expecting a few friends in, and hope to be able to make it pleasant for you.

JOSH. Miss Hugh, you will please excuse me from accepting your grapes, as I am out of tune this evening.

FOR. I think he has got the heart disease. He has

all the symptoms of it; a rush of blood to the head, and a confused feeling there, attended sometimes with a choking sensation.

HANNAH. Shall I tell ma she may expect to see you this evening at our house?

JOSH. I must be excused, as to-morrow I start on a long journey, and shall need this evening for preparations.

HANNAH. It's too bad. Come and see us when you get back. I hope your journey may improve your health.

KATE. Esquire Earle, will you accept these simple flowers from my mother. You cannot have the same objection to them that you had to the grapes. Flowers are a very appropriate offering to an invalid.

JOSH. Please, Miss North, favor our poor friend Mr. Dewey with your ma's bouquet. He is so languishingly fond of flowers, and I am, unfortunately, blind to their beauty. I like cowslip blossoms, in the early spring, for greens, and dandelions too, if they are not old.

KATE. Excuse us. Good evening.

HANNAH. I trust we haven't intruded. Good evening.   [*Exeunt.*

FOR. Esquire Earle! The millionaire! And treat young ladies rudely.

JOSH. Rudely! These simpering, buzzing bees saw no rudeness in my words. If I don't hurry out of town, they will be after me again with their poesies. I shall bring Betsey back with me — the liking is the marrying; but then, there is a good old minister down in Tarrytown that will tie the knot for us. I'll be a man when I've Bets. in the house, calling, in her own strong way, "Josh., Josh." Come, go home with me, and write the pink-paper note; you are skilled in such things, and I am a perfect blockhead.

FOR. I will write the pink-paper note with pleasure; but first answer me one question. I am deeply interested in that nice feeling that you recommend me to cherish. Now, you have loved two ladies passionately within the last half hour is the love for both equal? Have you no choice?

JOSH. Friend Ford., you have put to me a mighty nice question. The thing is just like this: I look up into the clear sky; I see beautiful lights and shades playing there; I try to reach them, but I find there is altogether too much of earth about me to rise so high. I see a glorious star, I call it mine, but its brightness dazzles my eyes. An angel is given to me; I fancy I am in heaven, gather up my heavy boots, and timidly sit by her side. She speaks; I am choking; I find her atmosphere altogether too etherial for me. I am like a fish out of water, and flounder in the same way until I reach a stratum of air I can breathe freely in. Do you understand me? If you do, write my pink-paper note, then I'm my own man again, and can lock arms with Betsey Ann.

FOR. Come, then, let's hurry off before any more of the fair ones scent your track. [*Exeunt.*

SCENE THIRD.

GRANTVILLE AMES seated at a table, arranging notes and papers for a journey.

[*Enter* HETTIE.]

HETTIE. Dear brother, Grantie, how soon will you come down into the parlor? Every moment seems lost that you are not with us.

GRANT. (*rises.*) In fifteen minutes I will be there. I have almost everything arranged for my journey now.

HETTIE. Dear me! your journey. 'T is so sudden I can't bear to think of it. Why don't you wait until next week?

GRANT. If I don't take the vessel that goes in the morning, I should have to wait a long time for so good an opportunity again. Then, the sooner I go the sooner I shall be back. Keep up your courage, pet. Don't forget your promise; write me by every steamer, and tell me everything that occurs here.

HETTIE. But, Grantie, how lonely ma and I shall be without you! And pa away, too!

GRANT. O, not very; I shall write you often, and the time will soon pass. If you keep every little moment filled with some interest, they will all fly on swiftest wings, and I shall be back here before you miss me. I have given you my secret, take good care of it.

HETTIE. I 'll take care of your secret, and Myrtle too.

GRANT. That is a good sister. Keep Myrtle with you as much as possible; she is lonely there with her father; read to her all my letters, and tell me every-thing you can about her.

HETTIE. Shan't you write her, Grantie?

GRANT. I am not quite sure. I must see her some-way before I leave. I do n't know how to manage the affair. Can 't you help pull my candy, Hettie?

HETTIE. Yes; I will go and bring her home with me to pass the evening. I must run before it is any darker. Come down in the parlor soon. [*Exit.*

GRANT. Possibly she can manage this for me, but I do n't feel certain. The miserable old man there has stepped in between us, with his "*Never.*" Yet I will see my pet before I leave America. Forty Dr. Lanes cannot prevent it. I have n't seen her since that miserly letter sprang out of the dust.

[*Enter* MYRTLE LANE, *dressed in white, her hair in ringlets over her shoulders.*]

GRANT. (*takes her hand excitedly.*) The very air I breathe is alive with blessings. What good angel sent you here, Myrtie?

MYRTLE. 'T was not an angel, but plain Capt. Orson. He asked me to call in here and get a book that he left lying on the table. Now, which one is it?

GRANT. Did he tell you I was here waiting to see you?

MYRTLE. No, he said nothing about you; only asked me to call for his book, and he would stay with father while I was gone. Now, which book did he leave here?

GRANT. Truly, the Captain has not forgotten his early days, the dear, good friend!

MYRTLE. Please, Grantie, tell me which of these books belong to him, for I must hurry back and not keep him waiting.

GRANT. He has no book here, my dear Myrtie. He has sent you on a fool's errand, as far as the book is concerned. Forgive this; and I will bless the good Captain as long as I live, for playing this pretty joke on you.

MYRTLE. This is n't like him. What does he mean by it, Grant.?

GRANT. He means to lay me under everlasting obligations to him. Moments are flying; I must not waste them. You found me here gathering up my papers. Did you know I was going to start on a short journey in the morning?

MYRTLE. No; are you going to Southland again?

GRANT. Not to Southland, but very, very much farther than sunny Southland. I start in the morning for Europe.

MYRTLE (*starting*). No, Grantie; not to far-off Europe? Not cross the wide Atlantic?

GRANT. That is my purpose.

MYRTLE. And why? And why have you kept it a secret?

GRANT. I have but just decided to go. I have kept it no secret. The why I'll tell you this evening : where can I see you?

MYRTLE. At father's. Can't you come round there?

GRANT. Would your father be glad to see me?

MYRTLE. Of course he will; and if you are going to Europe in the morning, he will think it very strange if you do n't call and bid him good-bye. What makes you ask that question, Grantie?

GRANT. I had a good reason for it. Did n't you know he wrote me a letter?

MYRTLE. No; what letter did my father write you?

GRANT. O, Myrtie, you know I rocked you in your cradle. I fought for you then; with your permission I will fight for you now.

MYRTLE. It does n't look much like it, going off to Europe in this informal way. I suppose it was to give me this information that the Captain sent me for a book. Did he know you were here?

GRANT. Of course he did. Captain Orson is pulling candy for me, and I will bless him as long as I live. He is converting an iron rod into a golden sunbeam. Myrtie, the Captain says you are his pet. He speaks boastingly of a power he has to control your destiny.

MYRTLE. He has made a pet of me all my life. I think he rocked me in the cradle earlier than you did. You know my beautiful shells and interesting curiosities; he brought them all to me from some foreign country. He has had my photograph taken annually, ever since I was a year old. 'T is true, I am his pet.

GRANT. You make me jealous of him.

MYRTLE. Well, that 's funny. I am jealous of him too; he was in the secret of your going abroad before I was. I do n't like it at all.

GRANT. This evening I will explain all to you. I think Hettie is at your house now, to invite you home with her. Can 't you pass the evening with us?

MYRTLE. I had forgotten; I promised Capt. Orson to

pass the evening at his house. He is going to send his carriage for me.

GRANT. Capt. Orson again! This is all right, I am invited there too. But what claim has he on you, Myrtie?

MYRTLE. The claim of a long and true friendship. He seems almost as near to me as father does. When ma was living, he was at our house a great deal. Ma always treated him like a brother. He was with her when she died, and I heard him whisper to her then, " I will watch over your darling "—and he has. He knows pa is full of business, and is from home a great deal, so he just comes and puts his bushy head in at the door, and sings out, " Myrtie;" if I am busy, I answer, " Here, Captain." " All well?" he inquires; and when I say " Yes," he rides off.

GRANT. There is a pretty romance in his devotion to you, Myrtie. I like it, yet am half afraid. Is there not a mystery about it?

MYRTLE. Not much. All know Capt. Orson has heaven in his heart; there is love there for everybody. He is alone in the world; has neither brother or sister, no wife nor chick; so he pets your baby. (*She takes her handkerchief out of her pocket, and a small, pink note falls to the floor. Grant. picks it up and gives it to her. She laughs, and blushes.*)

GRANT. And you are *my* baby? These flying reports; are they false?

MYRTLE. What will you give me, Grantie, if I will read this *billet-doux* to you?

GRANT. All that I call mine, with one exception.

(She opens it and reads.)

" MISS LANE: To relieve you and myself from further embarrassment, I write you this pink note. I am aware that the liking is more than half the marrying, and I like you mighty well, and all the better for your shyness. My liking is strong enough for the marrying, but yours, trembling bird, is not; and I yield, to a more favored wooer, all the claim to your white hand that your father bestowed on me. I know you are a true woman, and have the "blessed feeling" for somebody, and I advise you . to wait. With profound respect,

JOSHUA EARLE."

(Both laugh.)

GRANT. Myrtie, do tell me what made your father do such a foolish thing?

MYRTLE. Excuse him, Grant.; 't is the only foolish thing he ever did in his life.

GRANT. Not yet. I have his letter in my pocket.

MYRTLE. Read it to me; exchange is fair.

GRANT. 'T would hardly be in this case; but I will read it to you some time — not now. We will have no clouds this evening.

MYRTLE. I think my devoted friend will get tired waiting for his book; I have stayed too long.

GRANT. No; your worshiper is making a special contract with your father; your presence would embarrass them, believe me.

MYRTLE. Not a bit of it will I believe. I see you are curious about the Captain's interest in me. He has had his romance; I do not know much about it. It is in a written manuscript, sealed. He says it is for me when he closes his eyes in a long sleep; and he says he shall leave me other treasures that I must take good care of. I never question him. I think ma knew all, but she only told me a little. She had a sister, Myrtle — I was named for her. Ma said I was just like her. This Myrtle, Capt. Orson loved. There is a mystery and a sorrow about it unrevealed. Now, Grantie, good-bye till we meet at the Captain's.   [*Exit.*

GRANT. A mystery and a sorrow; yes, I believe it. The world is full of mysteries and sorrows. Life is a mystery, and sealed with many seals, which a little child only can open.

[*Exit, with his arms full of books and papers.*

A GOLDEN WEDDING.

Characters:

MR. *and* MRS. DUNLAP,
ELI, JAMES *and* SUSIE DUNLAP, *their Grandchildren,*
MAUD CLIFTON, *a Granddaughter.*

[GRANDMA *and* GRANDPA.]

GRANDMA. This dumb old crutch! now see, Grandpa, if you can keep it to yourself. I suppose I have tumbled over it, in my lifetime, some ten thousand times. Well, this is a sorrowful world, let people say what they will; the doors all squeak on their hinges; they are never iled.

GRANDPA. I think if you had a little ile on your tongue, Grandma, we should n't have so much squeaking.

GRANDMA. Now, Grandpa, hold back your wearisome philosophy; 'tis ill-timed. I would as soon stumble over your blamed old crutch as to listen to one of your lecterizing lecters. They affect me just like the galvanic battery. They set my nerves all on the jump. And now, Grandpa, if you want to do anything, just keep still. Susie, when did your Cousin Maud write us she would be here?

63

SUSIE. 'Tis to-day she is coming; and I expect her every minute.

GRANDMA. You do, do you? You look like it, with your old ragtag of a dress on! Why don't you go and fix up, instead of sitting there mending your gran'ther's stockings?

SUSIE. Grammie, I am fixed up. (*Rising.*) Doesn't my hair look nice? See how smooth I have combed it!

GRANDMA. Your hair looks well enough; but then, your old ragtag dress,—and sure as your gran'ther's crutch lives, you have on Jim's shoes!

SUSIE. I know it, Grammie; Jim said I might wear them when Cousin Maud came. You know mine are all worn out. Then these fit so nicely. (*Holding up her foot.*)

GRANDMA. *Fit you*, do they? They are big enough to put your gran'ther's crutch into; and I wish it was there, then may-be the doors wouldn't squeak so much on their hinges.

GRANDPA. A little ile on your tongue might make the doors turn easy on their hinges.

GRANDMA. Now, didn't I tell you to keep still if you wanted to say anything? If you will take care of your crutch, 'tis all I ask of you. But, Susie, why don't you fix up before your cousin comes?

SUSIE. Grammie, I have no better clothes than these; and I think as they are clean, Cousin Maud will like them; and then they fit me so well.

GRANDMA. They fit you as well as Jim's shoes do! I wonder who they were made for?

SUSIE. They were made for Peggy Fatfoot. But,

Grammie, do n't clothes always fit well when they are big enough? See here! I can turn 'round in them. And then, you know, I just put this red ribbon on to show Cousin Maud I have done all I could for her. I want she should love me, for I love her so much. Jim says she is an angel of a lady.

[*Enter* JIM.]

Now, Jim, tell us something about Cousin Maud; you have seen her?

JIM. Yes; and what shall I tell you?

SUSIE. Tell us who she is like.

JIM. She is like Grammie — all sunshine.

GRANDMA. Now, boy, stop your insults, or you will feel your gran'ther's dumb crutch about your ears.

JIM. Grammie, I did n't mean it as an insult. You know there is warm sunshine in your heart — only hidden by clouds.

SUSIE. Come, Jim, tell us about her; is n't she a lady?

JIM. Not as much of a lady as my pet Susie; but she dresses elegantly, and has a mint of money.

SUSIE. I am glad of that, Jim, for money is a good thing; and I like elegant dresses; their beauty reminds me of roses and lilies; but then they are not as pretty. The Bible says that even Solomon in all his glory, was not arrayed like the lilies. Do her dresses fit her well? You know, sometimes the dressmakers make them so tight that the ladies suffer most awfully. I hope she do n't wear her dresses so long that we shall tread on them when we kiss her. But, Jim, is n't she an angel of a lady?

JIM. Not so much of an angel as my dear Susie.

GRANDMA. Now, stop your nonsense, Jim. My heart is just breaking to have Susie appear in that rag-tag of a dress. She says she has no other. This is true enough. But, child, put on my go-to-meetin' dress! You shan't disgrace your family in this way. Put away your gran'ther's old stockings, and fix up!

SUSIE. Grammie, Cousin Maud will not look at my dress. She will look straight down into my heart.

JIM. Bravo, my darling sister! That is what Cousin Maud will do; and she will see more living beauty there than her eyes ever rested on before. But, were not these brawny hands of mine tied, I would clothe you in a way worthy of your own pure life. Things are as they are. It will not always be so. Now it takes all my wages to pay the rent of this old tumbling house, with the wood-bill and many other minor bills. When Eli comes home things may go better.

SUSIE. And do you know I expect him this very day?

JIM. And what makes you?

SUSIE. I feel such joy in my heart, I know he will come. [*Door-bell rings.*

[*Enter* ELI *and* COUSIN MAUD.]

GRANDMA (*tumbles over the crutch*). The dumb old crutch! But welcome, my boy — welcome, although trouble is here — your gran'ther's crutch is still living! but how do you do? Not lame, I hope!

ELI. I am well, and I have brought home with me Cousin Maud.

GRANDMA (*embraces*). Maud Clifton, my dear child!

You are my own Maud's daughter, and your Grandma welcomes you to her humble home. I have a world of things to say to you; but first speak to Susie. She has on her ragtag of a dress; but do n't look at it. I tried to have her put on my go-to-meetin' one, so she would look like somebody; but she 'd rather mend her gran-'ther's old stockings. Now you have spoken to Susie, speak to your poor gran'ther. I 've just got him to keep still, as that is the only way for him to say anything. And here is Jim. Now speak to him, though he do n't deserve it, as he is forever insulting his grammie. Now these tiresome ceremonies are all over, let 's know something how things come 'round in this way. Eli, how did you happen to pitch upon this gay bird?

ELI. 'T was my good fortune. We met, accidentally, in the cars.

GRANDMA. How did you know so fine a lady?

JIM. He knew her by her resemblance to you.

GRANDMA. Stop your wearisome nonsense, Jim! Well, I must admit, notwithstanding that blamed old crutch, there is some good luck in this fretting world. Maud (*taking her hand*), you must be dumbstruck to find us in this way of living; but do talk and tell us something. Some time ago, when you were living in Cuba, we heard you were almost dead.

MAUD. That was true, Grandma.

GRANDMA (*tenderly embracing her*). *Then 't was true!*—you *were almost dead!* The sun and moon be praised that you did n't *quite* die. I was thinking about a mourning dress for Susie when we heard that sad news. But, tell us, how did it happen? (Eli, excuse

my talking first to Cousin Maud; you know I ha'n't ever
seen her before.) But, child, how did it happen? The
story came to us that you almost died of *love ;* and that
is dreadful, you know; we shed many tears over it.

MAUD. Well, Grandma, you did'nt get the story
right. I came near dying for want of love.

GRANDMA. What do you mean, child? They said
Count Vantasi deserted you on your bridal day.

MAUD. He did, Grandma, and as you heard, I almost
died; but it was not with *love ;* it was with grief, mor-
tification, and anger. I shut myself into my private
room, and saw no one but my servant for three months.
I was vexed. I was terribly angry that Regal Vantasi
should dare to trifle with Maud Clifton; and I vowed
vengeance on his heartless head. Oh, those were dark
days that I passed in that lonely room! But they came
to an end — night with all its terrors gave place to
morning — and my life now is an unclouded day; it
knows no sorrow.

ELI. We can readily believe this, Cousin Maud, for
your happy face tells the story. But how the change
was wrought, from so dark a night to so bright a day,
we cannot conceive.

GRANDMA. This is true, Eli; and now I'll put your
gran'ther's crutch out of the way and listen to Maud
while she tells us how that terrible thunderbolt was
turned into perpetual sunshine.

MAUD. Weary of my solitary room, I wandered
forth, one morning, into a beautiful grove. I seated
myself upon a mossy bank, meditating upon the heart-
lessness of the world. I was weary, and fell asleep.

And now passed before me three panoramic views. The first was Regal Vantasi, counting two piles of money. One, I saw, was mine; the other, Reina Burgess'. Reina's was the larger pile; and I saw my old lover take this pile and walk off. This Reina was the lady he married.

ELI. We understand what that view means, very well. Now give us the second one.

MAUD. 'Twas Maud Clifton herself, dressed in the very bridal wreath she had prepared for her wedding. She stood admiring Vantasi's stately mansion, his long retinue of servants, and elegant equipage of horses, carriages, etc.

JIM. Well, what did you think of this scene? Did it satisfy your loving heart?

MAUD. It satisfied me there was no true love lost in the long and dark night through which I had passed. I ceased to blame Count Vantasi, while I rejoiced that I was not his wife.

GRANDMA. I don't cease to blame him. I will blame him as long as your gran'ther's crutch lives.

MAUD. But you see, Grandma, our love was cast in the same mould. We did not love each other. We only loved some good, real or imaginary, that we might gain by the marriage.

GRANDPA. Well, child, go on with the third picture; your old gran'ther is getting interested.

GRANDMA. Keep quiet if you 've anything to say!

MAUD. The third picture was beautiful beyond description. 'Twas an angel, with golden stars about her head. She was standing in an arbor of roses. I drew near to her, and she placed her hand upon my head, saying, in soft, musical tones: "My child, you are saved from a life of misery. Now, listen to me: Love never seeks its own good. Its very life consists in giving itself, with all it has, to another. It lives to bless; and in blessing it finds that pure and satisfying happiness that only angels feel." I awoke.

GRANDPA. And what next? Maud, you interest me.

MAUD. I began life anew. I sought for that love that blesses others. I clothed myself in the most simple attire, and went among all the poor and suffering people I could find. I sympathized with them, and tried to do them good. I cannot tell you all I did for them; neither can I tell you the needed rest and quiet happiness that followed it.

JIM. Yes, Maud, you can tell all; tell us everything you did, and what came of it! Did you find another Vantasi?

MAUD. Not another Vantasi; and I could not, since I was not the same silly, selfish Maud that found him in former days. I found, now, an angel instead of a demon, and I love him for himself. I love his pure, noble, disinterested spirit. I love his clear intellect. I can appreciate his fine taste. My heart grows in his atmosphere. But you smile, Jim.

JIM. Well, talk on! I like to hear you. This smile does n't mean anything. I was only fancying myself this wonderful hero, and a beautiful lady, with a hundred thousand dollars, kneeling and worshiping at my feet. In my weakness, I should accept her as sure as day follows night. I have no doubt the heart of this valiant knight of yours is full of love — I mean love of some kind.

GRANDMA. Jim, stop your nonsense! You shan't trifle with your Cousin Maud in this sinful way!

JIM. Grammie, I was only explaining the meaning of an innocent smile that came of itself, and Maud noticed it. I congratulate this fortunate man, and wish I stood in his boots.

SUSIE. No you do n't, Jim; and do n't talk so; you do n't want any better boots to stand in than your own. Search the world over, their equal is not to be found.

JIM. My dear, poor Susie — I will quote Cousin Maud's words — " my heart grows strong in your atmosphere!" You are a precious diamond set in earth's roughest clay. But this miserly setting does not tarnish the purity of the gem. I feel a power in the very marrow of my bones equal to create a better surrounding for my loving sister.

SUSIE. Jim, do n't talk in this way. I 've got things enough; and I 'll work to help you take care of gran'-ther and grammie; and you know they are all we have to see after. Eli can take care of himself, and Cousin Maud has everything she wants.

ELI (*stretching himself up very tall and laughing*). I hope I can do a little more than take care of myself. I have not been idle these three years. I have finished learning my trade. 'T is a good one. I can convert it into a pile of money. Jim will find he has an arm to help him, now I have come home. We together can clothe you in silks and satin, my Susie, and give you

nice slippers.   I should think those you have on were
rather too large and heavy for a gentleman's daughter
to wear!

SUSIE.   Eli, these shoes are Jim's; but then they fit
me nicely (*holding them up*); they are easy to my feet.

JIM.   My smile interrupted Cousin Maud.   Now let
us listen again to her interesting story.

MAUD.   Well, Jim, my hero does not know that I
have any money.   He believes me poor, like himself;
and *he* is entirely dependent upon his art and industry,
not only to support himself, but two orphan sisters
beside.   He is an artist, standing on the topmost round
of the ladder of his profession.   You see him early and
late, with his pencil and brush.   He has a fine percep-
tion of the beautiful; and, beside this, he has a proud,
independent spirit.   He loves to *give* much better than
to receive.   He thinks he can support me like a lady,
besides his two sisters.   I have deceived him.   He thinks
me poor; so you see I am in a difficulty.   I don't know
what to do.

JIM.   Let me help you, dear Coz.   'T will give me
pleasure to relieve you.   I know a pretty girl that
would be willing to share your money with me.   Will
you let us do you the favor?

MAUD.   You are too good, Cousin Jim.   But I will
tell you the plan I have in my mind.   'T is this: To
give all my money to grandpa.

JIM.   That is a grand plan.   I like it.   Now, Grandpa,
you will remember me?

GRANDPA.   I will hear the child's orders before I
promise to remember anyone.

MAUD. Well, Grandpa, I will put my property all into your hands. I have my papers with me. When Count Vantasi was my suitor he turned from me because my pile of money was too small. That has proved well. But I must take good care that my noble Henrike does not turn from me because the pile of money is too large.

JIM. Your style of talking is unique, Maud. You are original as our grammie is.

GRANDMA. Hush up, Jim! Maud, please go on! your gran'ther is quiet, but he feels interested. I would n't wonder if this affair should strengthen him up so much that he would walk without his dumb crutch. But we won't talk about his crutch now, since things seem brightening up. Jim, put your fist in your mouth! Now, Maud, what else?

MAUD. Well, I will give all my money to grandpa, and when Henrike and I are married, and have enjoyed love in a cottage long enough, I want he should buy us General Barton's elegant mansion. The General's grounds and shrubbery, you know, are very beautiful. I want them all. Grandpa, will this be asking too much of you?

GRANDPA. No, my child. To serve you in this way, or any other, will give me a taste of youth again.

MAUD. I want you should send a deed of it to Henrike in the most secret manner possible. Just write upon the margin: "A gift from the all-loving and all-wise Providence." He must never know from whence it came. I want him to stand in his relation-ship to me — *the giver*. He will like it better, and so shall I. You may buy the place as soon as it is conven-

ient for you; but do not send the deed until you have
a quiet sign from me.

JIM.　I'll bet, Cousin Maud, you do not keep that
secret two days after your fortunate lover receives his
magnanimous present.

MAUD.　I shall never tell him until we are so closely
united in love that we do not know the one from the
other — 'till all mine is his, and his is mine. (*Opening
her valise, and taking out a picture, gives it to grandma.*)
This is Henrike's likeness. 'T is his painting, too. He
sent it to you for a present. He said it was the best
thing he could do, next to coming himself. How do
you like it?

GRANDMA (*puts on her spectacles, looks at it, then
gives it to grandpa, around whom they all gather*). He
does n't look grand enough for you, Maud; but then I
suppose he will answer, if you like him. The liking is
the main thing. That's what I married your gran'ther
for, and I never repented the day.

MAUD.　Grandma, do you think I like Henrike?

GRANDMA.　Your manner of talking and doing things
seems kind of like it.

MAUD (*opens her valise again, takes out a beautiful
wreath made of orange blossoms, and puts it on grandma's
head, over her large ruffled cap*). This is a wreath to
crown your wedding-day.

GRANDMA.　My *wedding-day*, child! That day,
with all its glowing light, has long since passed, and
the blamed old crutch, with many a heartache, has
come in its place.

MAUD.　But this is your golden wedding-day, Grandma, and here is a purse for you. It will buy you that pretty cottage near General Barton's, and we will live side by side.

GRANDMA. Maud, Maud! Well, things are getting golden. Susie, I will give you that red dress that I wear to walk out in. But what shall we do with your gran'ther's crutch?

MAUD. O we will take the good old crutch with us, and in your new home you will learn to step lightly over it.

GRANDMA. And 't is a good old crutch (*picks it up*). It has been a dead and dumb thing fur me to fret over. Many times it has saved your gran'ther's feelings. I've never fretted at him, good man.

JIM. And the crutch has been a good thing to hold over my head, Grandma!

GRANDMA. But it never hurt you.

JIM. Only frightened me terribly.

GRANDMA. Maud, this purse is too much fur me. I am a poor sinner. Give it to your gran'ther if you have the heart to give it to anybody.

MAUD. In giving it to you, I give it to him; you and Grandpa are one.

GRANDMA. When the crutch is n't between us.

MAUD. And we will have the crutch changed to gold; then it will stand between you no more. Troubles and crosses patiently borne, only serve to make you more and more one.

GRANDMA. I understand your lesson, Maud. Maud Clifton is my own Maud's daughter. She teaches me to bear the trials of life patiently, and they will become blessings. Well, your old grammie will fret no more. If she can't step lightly over the crutch, she will walk around it. Susie is crying, sure.

SUSIE. No, I'm not crying, Grammie; the tears only blind my eyes. I am so glad for you and gran'ther.

GRANDMA. You may be glad, chicken; for you will have an egg in the nest.

JIM. And shall I, Grammie?

GRANDMA. Jim, now your gran'ther and me have become so suddenly rich you may stop bothering us.

JIM. Then I would be the same as dead.

GRANDMA. Go on with your nonsense, then; I can bear that better than your death; but you have got a few drops of blood in your veins that are a leetle too high colored.

JIM. The neighbors all say, Grammie, that I am like you.

GRANDMA (aside — Well, I did use to like fun). Now, Susie, go to my drawer and get that pair of black silk gloves! I'll give them to you.

MAUD. Keep them, Grandma! I am going to take Susie under my particular care. The diamond that stands in Jim's shoes may cast them aside. I will see to her setting. I will take care of her; and Jim and Eli may save their hard-earned money to share with the patient lasses that are waiting for them.

GRANDMA. That's good luck for the boys; for it's been hard on them to take care your gran'ther and me. To be sure, they would heir our property; but then that's in the future. Jim, you had better go 'round, this evening, and tell Angeline Meadows that we have become suddenly rich. She will feel so interested, you know. And there is little Betsey Hopper, that you use to spark about, Eli. She has grown to be a splendid lady. You can't go to see her to - night; but when we have seen you some, you can go. We have been so taken up with Maud that we have n 't looked at you at all. Do n't feel neglected, Eli.

ELI. Not a shadow of it. I have been taken up from the earth too. Your golden wedding has proved a great day for us, Grandma.

GRANDMA. Yes, I had no idea what a golden wedding was ; but few people live to see it. The sooner you secure your mate, Eli, the sooner yours will come 'round. 'T is a wonderful thing ! I could never have dreamed of it. But Maud has done it. She is a noble child. She is an angel. My blood is in her veins, and she do n't disgrace it. Maud has changed your gran'-ther's crutch to gold. Happy days are coming. Susie, let us sing ! Gran'ther's crutch is running ! Ding, dong, ding !   [*Curtain falls.*

THE DANDY PRINCE.

Characters:

MRS. BOULDERS, *a poor Widow.*
ANNA NICHOLS ⎱ *her Grandchildren.*
FANNY NICHOLS ⎰
JOB LAYTON, *Mrs. Boulders' Friend.*
ELSEY GREY.
NAT GREY.

MRS. BOULDERS, alone, seated, with her spectacles in one hand and snuff-box in the other. Dress, shabby and antiquated.

MRS. BOULDERS. If Mr. Scraper sets me into the street, he sets me there — that's all there is of it. I can't pay my rent — I've nothing to pay it with. Patty do n't send me any money; she knows the month has come round. I s'pose she has forgotten her poor ma. My dear boy, Zeke; when his letters came, Mrs. Boulders lived, not in this cobweb shanty, — she lived in a house, and had tea to drink. My boy, Zeke! If the good God would let me know where his head rests 't would lighten up my troubles a deal. But, as I said in the beginning, if Mr. Scraper sets me into the street, he sets me there; 't is n't so bad as being thrown out of the window. I shall see more of heaven's sunlight than I see in this room. He will have a pretty good lift to get me down stairs, but I shan't fight him any.

[*Enter* ELSEY.]

ELSEY. Grandma, what shall I get you for your supper ?

MRS. B. I have *only ten cents.* Strange, how riches are heaped up in piles for some fat bones to feast on, while many hungry ones are starving. How is your ma ? Has she anything for her supper ? If she has n't I will divide my stew with her.

ELSEY. Ma has so much pain to-day, she can 't eat any supper.

MRS. B. That is good—pain is a comfort to keep one from starving. But, my poor Elsey, have you anything ?

ELSEY. Do n't worry about me, Grandma; I can do well enough. I am young, you know; and when I 've nothing else to eat, I suck my fingers.

MRS. B. Yes, you are *young*, and it almost breaks my heart to see poverty pinching the bud. It do n't hurt me : my thread is almost spent. Elsey, poor child, there is none of my blood in your veins, but you call me *grandma.* That word, and the kind way you speak it, keeps me alive. My own have deserted me ; you have stood 'twixt me and death ; and yourself a poor child with a sick ma to take care of.

ELSEY. Do n't fret, Grandma ; something good will come to us. I 'm not hungry. The Shepherd will take care of his flock.

MRS. B. You blessed child ! Your pious talk has brought comfort to my aching heart many a dark night. Take this ten cents and buy for you and me ; it must make our supper and breakfast. After that, I 'll want no more.

ELSEY. What do you mean, Grandma?

MRS. B. I mean, Mr. Hardbones is going to set me into the street to-morrow; and if he sets me there, he'll set me there—I shan't fight him.

ELSEY. I'll fight him, and Nat will fight him. Mr. Scraper shall never set you into the street—never—never.

MRS. B. If he sets me there, he'll set me there. All my little duds here I'll give to you.

ELSEY. He shall never set you there, Grandma. The very earth itself would cry against it; 't would open and swallow him up.

MRS. B. I do not think it would cause an earthquake. My old bones might quake some. I hope he won't let me fall on the stairs.

ELSEY. Grandma, do n't speak such a thing again. I'll not let Nat go away to look for jobs to-morrow. We'll guard your door. Mr. Scraper! He is *Hardbones*. We'll throw him into the street—'t will do him good.

[*Enter* FANNY *and* ANNA NICHOLS, *gaily dressed.*]

FANNY. Does Mrs. Boulders live here?

MRS. B. She does.

FANNY. Can I see her?

MRS. B. If you open your eyes you can.

FANNY. (*Aside.* Good gracious! this can't be grandma.) Are you Mrs. Boulders?

MRS. B. I use to be Mrs. Boulders in my better days; I'm nobody now. To-morrow I am to be set into the street. If Hardbones sets me there, he'll set me there. But you, fine birds, have mistaken the door : pass along to your kind — there is nobody and nothing here for you.

(ANNA *covers her face.*)

FANNY. (*Aside.* What did ma send us to such a place as this for ?) We want to see Mrs. Boulders.

MRS. B. She is n't at home. To - morrow you 'll find her in a large garden, ready to receive her friends. If Hardbones sets me into the street, he 'll set me there.

FANNY. Do you remember your daughter, Patty ?

MRS. B. To be sure I remember her. She was a good girl to me once ; she has forgotten her poor old ma now, and her lonesome heart is breaking. If he sets me into the street, he sets me there — I shan't fight him.

ELSEY. (*Aside.* I 'll fight him ! He shan't do it.)

ANNA. (*Takes Mrs. B.'s hand.*) Patty has n't forgotten you ; we are her children ; she sent us here to take you home with us.

MRS. B. (*Puts on her spectacles : she looks first at one and then the other.*) I do n't know as you are Patty's children — you look like strange birds to me. Where did you come from ?

FANNY. We came from New York city. Ma lives there, and she wants you to come and live with her. Will you go home with us to - night ?

MRS. B. (*Puts both hands to her head.*) It aches here. Set me into the street. Live in New York — Patty's children — I do n't know — go to - night — where is Mrs. Boulders ? I can 't find her. Elsey !

ELSEY. I am here, Grandma.

MRS. B. Give me a glass of water. Now I begin to

see again.   If you are Patty's children, what made you
come after your poor grandma in such trim ?

ANNA.   Don't you like our dress, Grandma ?

MRS. B.   It don't look like dress at all.   I didn't
dress my Patty so ; I made her life easy ; I didn't tie
anything on to her back.   Don't it make you tired ?   I
see, poor things, you can't stand very straight.

FANNY.   It's the fashion, grandma.

MRS. B.   You must speak loud ; my ears are getting
rusty.

FANNY.   I said it was the *fashion*.   In New York all
ladies dress so.

MRS. B.   I can't go home with you then ; my old
back isn't strong enough to carry any extra burden
that your Dandy Prince orders to be borne.   I've read
about this dandy tyrant in the newspapers, but I didn't
know my dear Patty lived under his terrible reign.
Why don't the people revolt ?

FANNY.   They don't want to ; they like it.

MRS. B.   Does my Patty like it ?

ANNA.   Yes, Grandma ; every lady likes it.

MRS. B.   Great thunder !   What is the world coming
to ?   And my Patty—my sensible Patty—likes it !
This tyranical dandy of yours is worse than old Hardbones.   Old Hardbones only asks what belongs to him,
but this dandy grinder would grind the life out of a
body, and without any good coming of it.   Does he
order your boots to be made in that way ?

ANNA.   In what way, Grandma ?

MRS. B.   Don't you see ?   Maybe he blinds the eyes
of his subjects.   He squeezes your toes into a vice and

sticks a long stopple under your heels. How do you walk ?

FANNY. We walk well enough.

MRS. B. You had better sit down. I han't got many chairs ; but you can sit on that box. Elsey, get that roll of corn plaster for the girls,—they 'll need it.

FANNY. Grandma, will you go home with us to-night?

MRS. B. I 've got corns now. I could n't wear such things on my feet. Then I 'd never have such a little butter spatter on my head, and a great cushion tied on behind. If I were young and lived in your country, I would raise an army of sensible women — I would be their general — and we would march on this dandy prince of yours ; we would n't leave a green feather in his head till he gave us freedom. Ameriky is a free country. Why do n't my Patty leave New York and move into Ameriky? I can't bear to have my gal suffer so much. (*She wipes her eyes.*)

ANNA. New York is in America, Grandma ; and we are all free there. We need n't dress so unless we choose.

MRS. B. That is the worst part of it. I knowed something about this awful tyrant before I see Patty's children. I read the newspapers, and I know this dandy prince addles the brains of his subjects. They believe what he says is a humane law. If he tells them to have a spike put through their ears, they all laugh, and say, how nice ! I 've heern tell how pretty young gals will sit still in a chair, and never move nor make any objection, while one of his learned subjects runs a spike through the ear. Ever see any of this brutality there?

ANNA. 'T is n't brutal, Grandma; it do n't hurt much.

MRS. B. (*Wipes her spectacles; then, with the help of her cane, raises herself on to her feet, and looks close to Fanny's ears.*) Well, the cow may jump over the moon now! My Patty's children! Elsey, help me into my chair again—there now—here I am safe. Take this ten cents, make it go as far as you can for you and me. If old Hardbones sets me into the street, he sets me there; I shall have my freedom.

ANNA. (*Takes her hand kindly.*) Grandma, go home with us. You can wear just what clothes you have a mind to.

MRS. B. Yes, that is possible, but not certain. My Patty had sense when she was with her ma; your dandy prince, it seems, has addled her brains; he might addle mine, but I do n't believe he would.

ANNA. No, he would n't, Grandma; you can wear what you have a mind to.

MRS. B. But then I must see my Patty and her children suffering martyrdom every day. Your grandma has a tender heart.

[*Enter* MR. LAYTON.]

MR. L. Does Mrs. Boulders live here?

MRS. B. Her shadow is here; she herself is being ground to powder between old Hardbones and the tyrant Dandy Prince. (*Puts her hands to her head.*) Elsey, get me some water. Would you like to see Mrs. Boulders?

MR. L. That is my express object in coming here.

MRS. B. (*Wipes her spectacles, and looks through them.*) I do n't know who you be, but you set my heart all a-jumping. Maybe you know something of my dear boy, Zeke.

MR. L. I do; I have brought you tidings from him.

MRS. B. (*screams.*) Elsey — Elsey — help me. (*She faints.* ELSEY *bathes her head with water, unties her cap strings.* ANNA *holds a bottle of hartshorn to her nose. She revives.*) Elsey, keep close by me.

ELSEY. I will, Grandma; I'll take care of you. Nothing shall hurt you.

MRS. B. You blessed child! Mr. ——, I do n't know your name — but your voice sounds kind of home-like. Maybe I 've seen you before?

MR. L. Have you forgotten your old friend, Job Layton?

MRS. B. (*She takes his hand and kisses it.*) Have I forgotten my old friend? Not by a wheat-field. The dandy prince has dressed your face after one of his whims, so I did n't know my dear old friend. You and my boy Zeke has played many an hour together, and now you have brought me tidings of him. Job, Job, I am glad to see you. Elsey, bring that box here for Job to sit on; here, close to me. I ha n't got many chairs. That long box, Patty's girls can sit on — 't will be some help to their poor feet.

FANNY. Our feet are well enough, Grandma.

MRS. B. These are Patty's girls, Job — (*Mr. L. bows politely to them*) — and this, Elsey, is the child that has kept life in my body these last days. Bring the chip basket, Elsey, and sit close by me; there, now we are all fixed, I am ready to hear tidings. I can bear any-thing. I 've worn this black string round my neck two

years, mourning for my boy. I know'd something had
happened to him 'cause he did n't send me anything.
But, Job, if I do n't stop talking, I shall never hear of
my poor Zeke.

MR. L. You have worn mourning for him two years?
'T was two years ago he was taken sick; one year ago
I found him, and stayed with him while he lived. His
last thoughts were for his mother.

MRS. B. Then my dear Zeke has gone to his pa.
Well, they were fond of each other. I 'll soon be with
them, too. My Patty won't miss me. I do n't know if
the dandy prince will let her wear a black string for
me —'t is just as well. Elsey and Nat can wear one.

[*Enter* NAT, *shabbily dressed.*]

Well, Nat, I am glad you have come; sit here, close to
me. I have n't but one chip basket.

NAT. I 've got my heels with me. (*Sits on his heels
close to* Mrs. BOULDERS.)

MRS. B. Now, Job, tell me all about my boy. This
Nat, here, is Elsey's brother. If any good comes to me,
they shall share it. If evil, I 'll bear it alone. If old
Hardbones sets me in the street, he 'll set me there, and
I 'll sit alone. If my boy has sent me anything, if 't is
but a penny, I 'll share it with these children. Speak
on, Job.

MR. L. Your son trusted all his papers to my care.
His business was a good deal confused; I have been a
year in getting it straightened; it is completed now,
and there is a small sum of money left for you.

MRS. B. O, Job! my old friend, Job! Is there enough
to pay you for your trouble and give me two dollars for

Mr. Scraper ? 't is his due for the last two months' rent.
'T will save him the trouble of carrying me down stairs.
I am heavy, and he might let me fall.

Mr. L. You have a pile of money, Mrs. Boulders,
and you deserve it.

Mrs. B. Job, take well your pay before you give
anything to me. Zeke was your friend.

Mr. L. My pay was given me by Zeke ; all that
was left was for you. These were your son's last words
regarding business matters : — " Job," he says, " friend
of my early days, my mines and all that is connected
with them I give to you ; the rest of my property you
must sell for cash and take it to my dear mother. Take
it to her yourself, and assist her in making herself comfortable with it." So here I am, at your service. Your
property is at your disposal. To - morrow I shall move
you from this old shell of a building to a home worthy
of the mother of Zeke Boulders.

Mrs. B. Will there be money enough to pay two
dollars to Mr. Scraper ? he is so impatient.

Mr. L. (*Throws a pile of bills into her lap.*) Here
is money enough to last you until I return to - morrow
for you, with a carriage.

Mrs. B. (*Wipes her spectacles.*) Job, can you spare
me all this ? Here is a two dollar bill, Nat ; take this
and run round to Mr. Scaper, 't will save him some
trouble. And this is a five, Elsey ; take it to your ma
as quick as you can ; perhaps 't will ease her pain, so
that she can eat some supper. Now, Job, those two
burdens are off my mind, tell me how much my dear
Zeke sent me, that I may know what I can do.

MR. L. That little roll of bills I gave you is some odd change that belongs to you. You have a hundred thousand dollars beside, to do just what you please with.

MRS. B. Job, Job, help me to do good. I am rich in my old age ; 't is but a short time I shall want money. I must do what good I can. I will give Elsey and Nat and their ma a nice home.

FANNY, Grandma, sha n't you remember your Patty and her children ?

MRS. B. To be sure I shall. Here is a five for each of you, to buy you some shoes without a squeeze at the toe and a stopple at the heel. Go home now, and tell my Patty that I shall never live in a country that is ruled by a dandy prince. Tell her to come to the land of liberty, and accept good sense for her guide, and we will share our goods together.

FANNY. Mr. Layton, did n't Uncle Zeke send anything to my mother?

MR. L. He spoke kindly of your mother.

FANNY. And sent her nothing ?

MR. L. He gave all to your grandmother. He said that was more fit — she might have the pleasure of doing what she chose with her own.

MRS. B. Go home, girls, and be sensible. Your grandma is a just and generous woman. My son knew what he was doing. The first thing I shall do will be to buy the freedom of my Patty and her children.

[*Curtain drops.*

THE SHENSTONE SOCIETY.

Characters:

PRESIDENT, SECRETARY, and TREASURER, with a Society of Boys and
Girls — the Girls dressed in white.

The motto of the Society, " Each for the Other," written in large, golden
letters, is suspended over the stage.   A table in the centre, with some
chairs. Curtain rises ; twelve little girls — some standing, some seated.

SYLVIA.   I am so glad they let little girls belong to
the Shenstone Society,   I think it is the best society in
the world.

MATTIE.   So do I.   We have such good times here.
I never enjoy myself so much anywhere else.

MARY.   I don't think our society is the best one in
the world.

SYLVIA.   Do n't you have a good time here Mamie ?

MARY.   Yes, I enjoy it very much, and I know we
all enjoy it ; but this does n't make it the best society
in the world.

BESS.   You are right, Mamie.   I think the Masonic
Society is better than our Shenstone ; then, the Temperance Society is better.   My mother used to belong
to the Abolitionist, and that is a great deal better,
because its object was to free the slave.

[*Enter* PRESIDENT, SECRETARY, *and* TREASURER —
take seats.]

SYLVIA. Miss Winslow, is n't our society better than
the Temperance Society?

MISS W., PRESIDENT. We will compare their merits.
What is the motto of the Shenstone Society?

MANY VOICES. "Each for the Other."

MISS W. Well, we all understand that this means
we are to live for each other. In all that we do, we
are to try to make each other happy; and should any
one of us become intemperate, it would frustrate all our
work. So you see it is superior to Temperance societies,
for it serves all their use, and does more.

BESS. Miss Winslow, it is n't as good as the old
Abolitionist Society was, is it?

MISS W. I think it is better. Let us hear our motto
again.

MANY VOICES. "Each for the Other."

MISS W. Do you not see, just in proportion as we
live our motto, we are doing a greater work than the
Abolitionist did? A member of our Shenstone Society,
with its motto so warmly alive in his heart that it comes
forth into every act of his life, could never hold a slave.
Our Shenstone Society is an Abolitionist society. It
commences its work deep, destroying the root of the
evil; we are slaves to self-love; our society is formed
for the purpose of abolishing this tyrannical power.

MARY. I understand it. If the slavemaster loved
and lived our motto he would never hold a slave in
bondage.

SYLVIA. I was right. Our Shenstone Society is the

best society in the world. If everybody loved our motto, I think we should have heaven on earth.

Miss W. We should, Sylvia; and if everybody loved our motto, we should have no more woes; we should need no prisons; there would be no inmates for an alms-house. Give Love an abiding place with us, and all evils flee far away, and heaven is here.

Sylvia. How delightful it would be to live in this world then. We should n't need to die to go to heaven, because it would be right here at home. Let us all be Abolitionists, and unite our forces against Self-love. Miss Winslow, is n't Self-love the captain that leads an army of smaller forces?

Miss W. Yes, Sylvia; Self-love is the head. Let us, in our Shenstone Society, concentrate all our energies against this evil, and we shall make good progress in the work of reformation.

Sylvia. Although our society is the best one in the world, we are too small to do anything in so great a work. We can only be happy here together.

Miss W. You are mistaken there, Sylvia. The efforts we make here, in our little society, will be felt throughout the world. Move a drop of water in the mighty ocean, and every sister drop feels a thrill.

Sylvia. I do not understand this.

Miss W. You can understand that one drop of rain, falling upon our dry and parched fields, does good.

Sylvia. A little good.

Mary. And many drops will do much good; but each drop comes by itself. So each of us, little Shenstone girls, will be a drop of rain, and do a little good. Is n't that the way for us, Miss Winslow, to do?

MISS W. 'T is the only way — each do what she can.

BESS. Miss Winslow, may I ask a question?

MISS W. Certainly; sociability is the right hand of our society. Ask what you please.

BESS. My father belongs to the Masonic Society, and he thinks it is the best society there is. Do you believe our Shenstone Society is as good as the Masons?

MISS W. I think it is much better. They do n't let little girls belong to the Masons, nor women either.

SYLVIA. That is selfish in them, is n't it?

MISS W. It appears so. If they have a good, they ought to share it with us.

> "Ceasing to give, they cease to have,
> Such is the law of love."

[Enter two little girls dressed in blue.]

BESS. Then, you know, they have a nice secret.

MISS W. So have we.

MANY VOICES. Do n't tell; there are strangers here.

MISS W. Mary, lead forward these little girls. 'T is Lucilla Day and Kittie Hoar; we are glad to see you.

LUCILLA. I want to join your society. I have brought ten cents, is that enough?

MISS W. That is enough for little girls; fathers and mothers, and aunties and uncles, pay twenty-five. Give your money to our secretary, Miss Barton, and she will give you the badge of our society. (*Presents the new member a blue ribbon, with the motto of the society written on it in gilt letters.*) The society may repeat to this new sister our Shenstone motto.

ALL. "Each for the Other."

MISS W. Will you, Lucilla Day, adopt this as your motto?

LUCILLA. I will.

MISS W. Does your little friend here want to join?

LUCILLA. She does; but she has n't any money.

MISS W. "Each for the Other" is our motto. Kittie Hoar wants to join our society. She has no money. Are there ten little girls present, that could each give her a penny?

MANY VOICES. I will—I will—I will.

MISS W. Those that say "I will," may raise a hand. I count seven; there are seven cents promised for Kittie. I shall feel very happy in giving the other three.

LUCILLA. I will give one. I did n't think to raise my hand.

MISS W. Then there is two left for me to give. Kittie can join our society next month, when her friends bring the money.

[*The Treasurer*, MR. RUSSEL, *rises.*]

MR. RUSSEL. Miss President, allow me to advance the money on my own responsibility. I will trust the honor and honesty of the little ladies that have pledged themselves, a month. (*Gives the money to Kittie.*)

KITTIE. Thank you.

MISS W. Kittie may pass the money to the Secretary. (*She receives the badge.*)

MISS W. The society may give again our motto.

ALL. "Each for the Other.'

MISS W. Does Kittie Hoar accept this as her motto?

KITTIE. She does.

MISS W. Perhaps you have heard that our society has a secret?

LUCILLA. We have; and we want to know what it is.

MISS W. Place each of you a hand in mine. That is right. Will you keep our secret safe?

BOTH. We will.

[*Enter a company of Boys.*]

MISS W. Good evening, boys. You are in time. We have just received two new members into our society. The secret is now to be revealed. Kittie and Lucilla may take their position in the middle of the stage. The girls may take hands and form a half-circle round them. The boys may take their position behind the girls. That is right. We could n't get along if we had n't *boys* belonging to our society. They make a fine back-ground for our delicate flowers; and a strong wall of defence, too. Lucilla Day and Kittie Hoar, if you feel willing to receive the secret of our society, and think you are responsible for its safe keeping, raise your right hand, and repeat our motto.

BOTH. " Each for the Other."

THE SECRERARY (*rises; she holds in her hand two sealed letters; gives one to each of the girls*). Kittie Hoar, the ten cents you have paid into this society as the fee of your membership, I have sealed in this envelope. I have done the same with yours, Lucilla. Now, answer my questions. Do you know poor Mrs. Lonely?

BOTH. We do.

MISS BARTON. Do you know where she lives?

BOTH. We do.

MISS BARTON. Do you know she is deaf and very poor?

BOTH. We do.

MISS BARTON. Do you know in one side of her house there is a hole for her cat to enter?

BOTH. We do.

MISS BARTON. To-morrow morning, before the sun rises, take these envelopes (they are directed to her) and slip them through the cat-hole. If you promise secrecy, raise your hand.

(*Both raise a hand — a general laugh, and the circle breaks.*)

BEN. DRAKE. Is n't our secret a good one, Lucilla? I think it is number one. Each of us has done the pretty deed you are to do to-morrow morning. Do n't be behind time; you will find a big company at the corner waiting to escort you on duty. You know Mrs. Lonely is deaf; there is no danger of her hearing us.

FRED. HUNT. 'T is fun to hear the old lady inquiring all over town about the mystery; but she do n't say much now. She finds it of no use — our secret is safe. She says the money that comes through the cat-hole, pays her rent and buys all her wood. You know there are over a hundred members, and we pay our fee annually, so she gets a good deal.

LUCILLA. I think 't is a good secret; but if the Shenstone Society gives all this money to poor Mrs. Lonely, what do they pay for the trees and flowers with?

MISS W. I will explain that to you. We have entertainments in this hall once a month; they are interesting; the room is crowded with listeners. All that do n't belong to the Shenstone Society pay twenty cents at the door.

KITTIE. What makes you let the members of the society in free?

MISS W. The members provide the entertainment.

KITTIE. I can't do anything.

MISS W. You are a good singer, Kittie. We shall let you join the Shenstone Glee Club.

LUCILLA. What can I do?

MISS W. You can take part in the dialogues. There are many ways here that you can make yourself useful. Next month our dialogue is "The Gold Snuff-box." You and Kittie can come then without taking a part in anything; wear your badge, that will give you admission.

KITTIE. O, I am so pleased to belong to the Shenstone Society. What fun we shall have!

MISS W. There is one thing more I must tell you. You have seen the Shenstone Park?

LUCILLA. I have walked in it a great many times.

MISS W. Did you notice the shrubbery and flowers there?

LUCILLA. I did; they look beautiful.

MISS W. Every member of the society plants a tree or bush there, and each takes care of his own, and in this way they are all taken good care of. Now, you and Kittie may plant there your favorite shrub; Miss Barton will show you your ground.

LUCILLA. I will plant a rose-bush—a moss rose-bush.

KITTIE. And I will plant a lilac. Will that do?

MISS W. Yes; plant what you like, and do nor forget to take care of it. The first evening of next month is a public entertainment. The middle of the month comes our social meeting like this. Now, you understand all about our society. Form yourselves into a circle again. What is our motto?

ALL. " Each for the Other."

MISS W. Now, if Mr. Russel will lead in music, we will have a good-night song.

(*All sing.*)

" Bright, rosy day has gone to her rest,
And covered her face with the shadows of night —
Shadows all gemmed with glittering stars,
And cheered by the beams of soft moonlight.
So we 'll sing her a song of sweet lullaby,
We will sing her a song of good-night ;
Good-night, rosy day — good-night, good-night,
Cheered with the beams of soft moonlight.

" Now, patient friends, go home to your rest,
Go, yield drooping eyes to the shadows of sleep —
Shadows all bright with innocent dreams,
And safe 'neath the watch that angels keep.
So we 'll sing you a song of sweet lullaby,
We will sing you a song of good-night ;
Good-night, patient friends — good-night, good-night,
Safe 'neath the watch that angels keep.

[*Curtain falls.*

BRINGING BACK THE SUNSHINE.

Characters:

MRS. DALE.   SAM CARTER.
DICK and BENNY, *her Sons.*   MRS. KEATS.
BETTY OAKS, *Mrs. Dale's servant.* MR. LOW.

[MRS. DALE *and* BENNY.]

MRS. D.   Now, Benny, my dear child, do n't trouble
yourself any more about the rabbits.   The first chance
your father has, he will buy you another pair.

BENNY.   Father is full of business, he will never find
another pair; besides, he can 't find any so pretty as
mine were.   Ma, what do you think became of my little
white bunnies ?

MRS. D.   I think they must have wandered off so far
that they did n't know the way back.

BEN.   That could n't be.   If they went off, we should
see their little tracks in the snow.   Some wicked boy
has taken them.

MRS. D.   Do n't think about your bunnies, Benny.
You have enough other things to amuse yourself with.

BEN.   I have n't much left now.   Some wicked man
drove his wagon wheels over my little wheelbarrow and
broke it; Dick cut off my horse's tail, and that is n't

98

pretty to look at; he spoiled Kitty, too, when he cut her ears off.

MRS. D. Do n't mind these things, Benny. You are getting to be a large boy; to-morrow you will be nine years old—almost a man.

BEN. I do n't want to be a man yet: and when I am, I hope I sha n't have as much trouble as I do now. Yesterday, you know, I was blind. My forehead is sore yet where I ran against the bureau, trying to find the door. Dick is a bad boy. I wonder what made him think to drop tallow from the candle on to my eyelids when I was fast asleep; then, when I waked up I could n't open them.

MRS. D. Dick does a great many things there is no accounting for. He is full of mischief; but then, he loves you, Ben; you know he made your wheelbarrow.

BEN. I know it, and it took him a good many days to make it, and that is what made me feel so bad when it got broke. I love brother Dick, and I wish he was a good boy; do n't you, Mamma

MRS. D. Dick is n't a bad boy, but he loves fun, and this oftentimes leads him too far. It leads him into mischief. But he is growing older, and will soon see the folly of it and correct himself.

[*Enter* BETTY, *with shawl on.*]

BETTY. Mrs. Dale, I have just come in to say that I am after leaving you. And I am breaking my heart, too. That boy Benny, I love more than myself; and the swate babie—I am dying to part with it. As I said, my heart is breaking.

MRS. D. Betty, you have been with me ever since I

kept house : 't is nineteen years. What has happened now, that we must part? Is your old friend, Mike, after you again ?

BETTY. No, missis, no ; I would n't go with Mike, he has too many childers. If I marry any man, it shall be a young one and good looking.

MRS. D. What is it, then ?

BETTY. (*Looking frightened around the stage.*) Your house is haunted. I have heerd noises before that scared me, but last night I seed the old fellow himself. I was so scared my hair jumped straight up and my knees jumped down. I was cowld as a gravestone.

MRS. D. What was it, Betty ?

BETTY. That is the question. The wisest of men can 't answer it. Nobody can tell what kind of stuff a ghost is made of.

MRS. D. O Betty, you are very foolish , there are no ghosts.

BETTY. I know you are a woman that spakes the truth always, but I must believe my own eyes first. I saw the awful, frightful thing. 'T was a graveyard ghost —all white.

MRS. D. If you saw anything, it might have been Dick, with a sheet over his head.

BETTY. 'T was no Dick, and no sheet. It was a very tall ghost : his head looked like a ball of fire.

[*Enter* DICK, *dressed as a ghost.* BETTY *screams and catches hold of* MRS. DALE. BENNY *is frightened and hides behind the door.*]

MRS. D. Dick, my misguided boy, when will you learn wisdom ?

[DICK *throws off his disguise.*]

DICK. Excuse me, mother; I did n't expect to find you and Betty here, and Benny too.

BETTY. (*Takes hold of his arm and shakes him.*) You wicked crather! You frightened the life out of my body last night. Dick Dale, if your soul was in purgatory, Betty Oaks would n't say masses for it. You are not your mother's son — you are a big bundle of mischief glued together to torment the life out of a body. (*She shakes him again.*) What do you say for yourself, you spongie tater?·

DICK. I say, I am so perfectly ashamed of myself and my meanness that I wish I was a veritable ghost, that could be annihilated.

BEN. Brother Dick, you are a bad boy; almost as bad as the one that stole my bunnies.

MRS. D. Dick, what did tempt you round here in this frightful dress?

DICK. My evil genii, Mother. I expected to meet Sam Carter here and frighten him a little, for fun. He will be here soon.

[*Enter* SAM.]

SAM. What is all this, Dick? Have you been playing the ghost?

DICK. Yes, Sam, and it was intended for your benefit. Mother, and Benny, and Betty have spoiled my fun.

SAM. Better have it spoiled this way than a worse one. I have in my pocket father's revolver; 't is loaded. I have always said I would shoot the first ghost I met.

BETTY. *Do it*, Sam, but do n't shoot Dick; spake first, before you let go your bang.

Mrs. D. My child do n't deserve this kind plea from you, Betty.

Betty. O, I would spill my own blood before I would have a drop of Dick's wasted.

Ben. Sam Carter, if you shoot brother Dick, I 'll knock you down.

Sam. Well, Dick, I do n't see but what you have friends enough, after all your mischief. Should I play half the tricks you do, I should be expatriated.

Betty. That is true ; for you are not clever like as our Dick is. I would never let anybody beside himself have a second chance of putting the cat into my dinner pot. He is a good boy. There is nothing under the earth, nor over it, that he can 't do. (*She catches holds of his arm, and shakes him with all her power.*) Dick, if I could shake the evil out of you, I would worship you as a saint. You are going to make some day my ideal of a gintleman, and when that day comes I wish Betty Oaks was a young lady. (*Shakes him again.*) I wish I could shake the devil out of you.

Ben. Do n't shake him so hard, Betty ; he made my wheelbarrow. Dick, to-morrow is my birthday.

Dick. I know it, Benny. Here is three dollars for you to buy Captain Gray's three rabbits ; they are prettier than yours were. I saw him to-day ; he said you might have them for three dollars.

Ben. I sha n't take this money, Dick : 't is some you have been all the year working for, to buy a fiddle with. I want the rabbits, but I will not let you give me this money. You are the best boy in the world, Dick.

BETTY. That is true of him.

DICK. I have the best mother in the world; the best little brother; and the best friend in Betty.

BETTY. You are so good yourself, Master Dick.

DICK. Here, Benny, take this money, and enjoy your rabbits.

BEN. I will not take it, Dick. Some wicked boy killed my rabbits, and I will do without them. Buy a fiddle with your money · I want something else of you for a birthday present.

[*Enter* MR. LOW.]

MR. LOW. (*Presents* MRS. DALE *a bill.*) Please give this to your husband; 't is a bill of fifty dollars for the damage done to my best cow. Some one tied a tin pail to her tail last night, and she was so frightened it has completely ruined her for milk. Your son's reputation is such that there is no question about the rogue. Good evening. [*Exit.*

DICK. I am innocent of this charge, Mother. He said it was done last night. Betty can testify that I was at home, entertaining her, then.

BETTY. I can testify to Dick's innocence in all things.

MRS. D. Dick, will you not learn a lesson now? 'T is your *reputation* that brings this charge upon you.

DICK. Mother, I am learning very fast this evening.

[*Enter* MRS. KEATS.]

MRS. KEATS. Mrs. Dale, can I see your son Dick?

MRS. D. This is my son Dick.

MRS. K. Master Dick Dale, my daughter Susie has a bad sprained ankle. Will there ever come an end to your playing tricks upon the school girls?

DICK.　I am sorry Susie has a sprained ankle.　Can I do anything for her?

MRS. K.　You can do as much as to pay the doctor's bill.

DICK.　Why do you expect me to pay the doctor's bill?

MRS. K.　Was it not you that challenged her for a race on that ice, on purpose to see her fall?

DICK.　How much is the doctor's bill?

MRS. K.　'T is one dollar.　I am a poor woman and cannot well afford to pay it.

DICK.　(*Gives her a dollar.*)　Will this exonerate me from blame in tempting your daughter to an ice-race?

MRS. K.　'T is the least you can do.

DICK.　I might call upon her, and, in person, offer my sympathy.

MRS. K.　Do n t mock us, boy.　　　　　[*Exit.*

BEN.　Dick, was that dollar some of the money you have been working so hard for all winter?　Was it some of your fiddle money?

DICK.　Yes, Benny, and here is three dollars of it for you.　Go, get those pretty white rabbits.

BEN.　I sha n't take your money, Dick.　The boy that stole my bunnies ought to get me some more.

DICK.　Good brother Benny, I am a mean boy.　I have been a hector to you ever since you opened your eyes to the light of this world, and yet you stand here to-night, with your baby fist, threatening to knock down big Sam Carter if he shoots my ghost.

BEN.　And I will; and Betty will help me.　Do n't you shoot brother Dick, Sam.

SAM. I should n't dare to, with *you* as his defender.

DICK. But, Benny, take this money —'t is your birthday present.

BEN. I do n't want such a birthday present from you, Dick.

DICK. What do you want?

BEN. I want you should bring back the sunshine.

DICK. Have I carried it away, Benny?

BEN. Yes, Dick. I have heard ma say that you took away all her sunshine. And when I go into the kitchen, and Betty can 't find her things in their place, and she goes for her glasses, and they are all stuck up with putty so she can 't look through them, she says, " That devil of a boy, Dick! he takes away all my sunshine." And when I put on my shoes of a cold morning, in a hurry, to get to the breakfast table as quick as father does, and feel little shot in the toes, so that I can 't walk, I say, " That devil of a boy, Dick! he takes away all my sunshine." Now, Dick, bring back the sunshine; bring back the sunshine for my birthday present.

DICK. How shall I do it, Benny?

BEN. (*Hesitates.*) Do n't play the devil any more.

DICK. I am so thoroughly ashamed to - night, I believe I shall never do it again. Benny, I am going to turn round. I will not take the sunshine away from the whole household again; and what I have taken away I will try to bring back. I know the wicked boy that murdered your bunnies. I know where he is now.

BEN. Where is he? Where is he, Dick?

DICK. Sam Carter has a revolver — he can shoot him.

BEN.　No, Sam sha n't shoot him; he *may* shoot him if he do n't pay me for them, so that I can buy some more.

DICK.　If he pays you for them, will you forgive him?

BEN.　Yes.

DICK.　Well, I am the wicked boy; and here is the money to buy more.

MRS. D.　Dick! Dick!

DICK.　I am not so bad a murderer as it seems. I shut them up, just to frighten Benny; then I went over to uncle's, and forgot to let them out; and when I came back they were dead. I was very sorry; and if Benny will forgive me this time, I will promise to bring back the sunshine as far as I can.

BEN.　And that is my birthday present. Sunshine for ma, sunshine for Betty, and sunshine for me.

DICK.　And when I bring any more clouds, let Sam Carter shoot me with his revolver.

BETTY *and* BEN.　No, no! Never, never!

[*Exeunt.*

———

THE SEQUEL.

BETTY.　(*Scouring knives.*) What an angel o. a boy our Benny is! Who but his pure self would ever think of asking such a birthday present—" Bring back the sunshine." And he asked it for his ma and Betty too. And what a wonderful deal of it Dick has brought! He was born a budget of fun, and he used to take it all to himself, robbing everybody about him of the comfort of life. Now he shares it so generously the house is full of sunshine ; he just keeps me laughing so much, I can hardly do my work. I should n't wonder if my hair turned red again. Then his ma — she is growing young every day, and she ought to. What a wonderful woman she is! She not only gave birth to the babyhood of Dick, but her long patience has made him over again. She has never knocked Dick round, as some mothers do their budgets of mischief. Many times she has said to him, " Dick, will you never learn wisdom?" How sorry the poor boy would look when he saw he had given the best of mas pain! And I believe Betty Oaks has helped him some in kicking away the devil. I never told all the tricks he played on me, and I never knocked him but once, and then I cried more than he did. Well, Dick Dale is the most remarkable boy there is in the country ; and I should n't wonder if he made the most remarkable man. He 'll never forget his friend Betty, and he ought not, for I have helped make him.

[*Enter* BENNY, *with a new sled in his hand.*]

BEN. Betty, did you ever see such a boy as Dick is? He has made me a sled.

BETTY. Benny, all these things come from your asking for that birthday present. How in the name of all the taters of Ould Ireland did you happen to think of it?

BEN. I wanted it so much I could n't help think of it. Now, Betty, we do n't have any more trouble, do we?

BETTY. Not a shadow of it. And then, Dick gives us just as many surprises as he use to ; but they are so different. You see, Benny, these warm overshoes he gave me? he bought them with some of his fiddle

money.   I found them one day, wrapped up in a paper,
in the dinner pot, where he use to put the old cat.

BEN.   I saw them, Betty.   But the sunshine that
he brings is the best of all.   I heard father tell ma last
night she was growing handsome.   She said, it was not
her fault, for she had so much sunshine she couldn't
help it.

BETTY.   Don't you think, Benny, I am growing
young, too?   Did you know Dick said he would invite
Mr. Screechy round here to see me?   And Dick never
tells a lie.

BEN.   Maybe he is down in the kitchen now; somebody is there, and wants to see you.

BETTY.   What kind of a looking man is he?

BEN.   O, he looks old as our old cat.   He has got no
hair on his head; he has got no teeth; he has got but
one eye; and he is lame.

BETTY.   That's him.   Why didn't you tell me he
was in the kitchen, and wanted to see Miss Oaks,
sooner?

BEN.   He said he was in no hurry.   Betty, he looks
awfully.   I wouldn't put my glasses on to look at him.

BETTY.   O, his looks is nothing, Benny.   Dick and
your pa both say he is a good man; and I am getting
kinder lonesome; and he owns a good cow, too.   But
I must go down.   If he isn't in a hurry, I am.
Benny, this is bringing back the sunshine of my early
days.   I feel so young; do I look well?

BEN.   Yes, Betty, you look like the sun itself—but
that ugly old man?

BETTY.   O, he'll turn into sunshine.   [Exeunt.

THE BUMBLEBEE.

Characters:

MRS. BUTTERS.
BETSEY, *her Grand-daughter.*
MR. NOIT, *a Stranger.*
SIX LITTLE GIRLS *dressed in white, and* SIX BOYS.

MRS. BUTTERS *and* BETSEY *on the Stage.*

MRS. BUTTERS.   This is a great day; 't is the seventieth anniversary in the history of Polly Onion, now Madam Butters.   Three-score years and ten is the measure of her days — honored indeed with such a long pilgrimage.   Two-score years and five she walked side by side with her good man, Tim Butters; and he was a good man, had only one fault — he liked to have his own way, and he would have it, in spite of Polly Onion. Well, that was manly in him.   I notice all men like to have their own way — and women.   Let them alone.   I gave Tim his share of trouble.   I hope he rests now. Betsey Butters, put away that book, and talk to your grandma.   This is her birthday.   It must be celebrated.

BETSEY.   I know it, Grandma.   I thought about it all day yesterday, and I know it will be celebrated, but I can 't tell how.   I had a dream last night.

109

Mrs. B. You did? Why did n't you tell me of it before you ate your breakfast?

Betsey. It will come to pass all the same, Grandma; it will come to pass I know, but I can 't tell how.

Mrs. B. Betsey Butters, I notice you have on your red dress this morning, and a red rose in your hair.

Betsey. And I notice, Grandma, you have on your green dress, and your cap with a wide ruffle and trimmed with green.

Mrs. B. I alers wears this green suit on my birthday — alers since your good grandpa died. I know what green signifies. I 'm not without hope — hope for some young joy in this world, and hope for lasting joy in the other. But, Betsey Butters, I do n't know what red signifies.

Betsey. It signifies love, grandma; and now you know why I wear it to - day.

Mrs. B. You love your grandma; well, that is a good thing, since you 've no pa and ma to love. But what about your dream, Betsey Butters? Let 's have it, even if 't is after breakfast. Your dreams are about as true as a bumblebee.

Betsey. I saw six little white lambs in your bedroom; you were asleep there on the bed. Your hair was bright and shining and laid in ringlets on your neck, and on the pillow; your cheeks were round and rosy; you looked beautiful, Grandma; just like a baby. The lambs played all round your bed; after awhile they jumped upon the bed and put their noses close to your face. Then you grew more beautiful, Grandma. They walked all over you, but they did n't wake you, for there seemed to be no weight to them. While I was looking at them, six white doves came into the room, and they kept flying about over your bed. Then I saw rainbow lights, and flowers all about the room.

Mrs. B. What else?

Betsey. Nothing more, Grandma. I tried to come and get into the bed with you, and that woke me.

Mrs. B. O, Betsey Butters, why did n't you tell me that nice dream before breafast?

Betsey. I did n't like to, Grandma. You looked beautiful; and the lambs, and the doves, and the rainbow lights and flowers. But you must n't go away yet, you must n't leave me alone. I am afraid of the dream.

Mrs. B. O, Betsey Butters, you need not be afraid of the dream. It is a nice one — better than the bumblebee. It do n't mean that I 'm going to leave you.

Betsey. What does it mean, Grandma?

Mrs. B. It means, I have a little grandchild on my birthday that is blessing my life with her pure innocent affections and bright heavenly thoughts. I smell now fragrant flowers and see rainbow lights.

Betsey. You make me glad, Grandma; for I was afraid of my dream, and the more so because last evening I saw the moon over my left shoulder; and this morning, when I first saw the cat, her tail pointed to the north.

Mrs. B. We will not mind those common signs; something may come of them, but nothing of any account. This morning, you know, when you went out to pick up some chips, you fell into the muddy ditch; we will balance that against the cat's tail pointing

northward. The signs from cats' tails never mean anything very exalted. Cats are of low origin. The goblet
you broke this morning was bad luck enough to square
off the account with the moon over your left shoulder.
These things done with, now lets look at the bright
ones. Your dream is being fulfilled every moment. I
am asleep as it regards all the cares and perplexities of
this world. I have taken a burden and yoke upon my
shoulders that is easy to bear. I feel about me innocent lambs, and I see white doves. Betsey Butters,
this beautiful dream of yours is enough to celebrate this
my seventieth birthday. Do n't you want some maple
sugar? There is some in the cupboard.

BETSEY. I cannot eat maple sugar to-day, somehow.
I feel as if something was going to happen.

MRS. B. Well, there will, Betsey Butters. There
alwers does on my birthday. Just seventy years ago I
celebrated the day, by coming into the world. Sixty-
nine years ago to-day I had my first tooth. I was lazy
about getting my teeth. Sixty-eight years ago to-day
my mother gave me a brother. Fifty years ago to-day
we had a great celebration — your grandpa and I were
made one.

BETSEY. What do you think will happen to-day,
Grandma? I know something will.

MRS. B. I count greatly on the bumblebee. I
never knowed one on 'em to tell a lie; and this one,
Betsey Butters, was a tremendous lively one; just as
quick as I opened the door this morning, he came buzzing straight into my face. I tried to drive him away,
but he would n't go; he kept buzzing close to one ear,

then the other, as if he were talking love to me. Some stranger will be here before night, I am sure. Let him come, we are ready, always ready, for whatever may come on my birthday. I hear a tapping at the door.

(BETSEY *opens it. Enter six little girls, dressed in white, each with a bouquet of flowers in her hand; six little boys follow, with small baskets on their arms. They form a half-circle round* MRS. BUTTERS. *The girls present their flowers: one of them says* —

Mrs. Butters, we knew it was your birthday, and so we brought you some flowers. Will you accept them?

(*The boys present their baskets, and one of them says* —

What the girls knew, they told us boys, so we followed in their flowery footsteps, and have brought you some fruit: please accept our offering.

MRS. B. Indeed I will. Blessed children! 't is such as you the Lord took in His arms when He was on earth. This is your dream, Betsey Butters.

BETSEY. I see it, Grandma, and we thank the good children very much.

MRS. B. Indeed we do. These gifts from my little friends delight me; they make feel young like them. Now, children, when your birthdays come round, send a pigeon's wing to Madam Butters. Will you remember it?

MANY VOICES. We will. [*Exeunt children.*

BETSEY. Grandma, this is the interpretation of my dream. But I still feel as if something else was to happen.

MRS. B. The bumblebee's stranger is to come yet. That will finish the day. Does my cap look all right, Betsey Butters?

BETSEY. Yes; and you look handsome, Grandma, for an old lady.

MRS. B. And you look handsome, for a young girl, Betsey Butters. I hear a tap at the door again—this is the bumblebee's stranger. Let him in.

(BETSEY *opens the door. Enter* MR. NOIT, *a tall, well dressed old gentleman.*)

MR. NOIT. Have I the pleasure of seeing Mrs. Butters?

MRS. B. (*Rising.*) I am Mrs. Butters. Please be seated, sir.

MR. N. Mrs. Butters, do you remember your old friend, Ethan Noit?

MRS. B. Indeed I do. (*Offers her hand.*) And I am glad to see him. This is my seventieth birthday. I was expecting you.

MR. N. That is pleasant. I thought to surprise you. Many years have passed since we met, and yet I see in Mrs. Butters, Polly Onion—the pretty girl that I loved in the freshness of youth. You are a widow now, I believe.

MRS. B. Yes, I have been a widow three years.

MR. N. And do you manage to keep life always cheerful?

MRS. B. With the help of my dear grandchild. This is Betsey Butters; she is the only child of my son Ethan Butters. She is a dear girl, and keeps my heart warm. I could not live without her.

MR. NOIT. I see in her dimpled cheeks and clear black eye something of Polly Onion. Impressions made on the plastic heart of youth never fade out. My Martha died two years ago ; since then I have passed many a lonely day. My children are all married ; I am alone. In the quiet evening hours, I live in the distant past. I sit on the mossy slope in the pale moonlight ; the air is laden with the sweet breath of the honeysuckle, rose and mignonette ; the wakeful katie-dids are making merry with their fiddles ; I sit upon the mossy slope, with the prettiest black-eyed maiden by my side that ever made Eden a paradise. (MRS. BUTTERS *wipes a coming tear.*) I see, dear Polly, the past is not all faded with you. Do you remember the sad moaning of a dove we heard that evening ?

MRS. B. I remember it well ; the sound has been too often repeated for me to forget.

MR. N. You believed in signs then, and half made me believe them too. Your influence over me in those days was wonderful. I heard the strange cooing of the dove, and that was all ; you interpreted it, Polly, but, I think, falsely. Still, you made me believe, and sent me away as one whom Heaven had banished from paradise. I have wandered long in the cold and dark — my heart hath found no rest, no home ; so I come back. Will you banish me again ?

MRS. B. Ethan, my thread of life is almost finished ; this is my seventieth birthday.

MR. N. I have counted your birthdays each year as they came. Polly, with my wife and my children, I could not forget you ; and the remembrance was no sin. I did what I could to make Martha happy ; I did what I could for my children. They have all left me. I am alone. Do you hear the sad moaning of a dove to-day, Polly ?

Mrs. B. No. 'T was my father's voice then. He had given me to Mr. Butters, and I was not *free*, and the dove moaned.

Mr. N. And you are free now, Polly?

Betsey. No, sir, she is not *free* now; she is my grandma; she belongs to *me*.

Mr. N. My dear child, I rejoice that she is your grandma. I would not separate her from you for all the gold in the mines of this earth. I only propose to be company to you and her. I will serve you both, in doors and out. I will keep a carriage for you to ride in, and a Darkie to drive you. Whatever Bessie wants, that money can buy, she shall have. Now, will you not leave your grandma free to act for herself? Do not make the dove moan again.

Betsey. Grandma is *free*. She is the only grandma I have. She must be happy. You must n't teaze her.

Mr. N. Pretty bird, I will not teaze your grandma. I teazed her once; it did no good; the dove moaned, and I was sent away. I only ask her if she will send me away again?

Mrs. B. I named my only boy, *Ethan Noit*. The Lord hath taken him from me.

Mr. N. Thank you, Polly, for that fond remembrance. Ethan Noit of your early days is with you again, repeating his heart's pleadings.

Mrs. B. Is it not too late, Ethan?

Mr. N. Never too late, Polly. True love never grows old. Let our last days be our happiest.

Mrs. B. Ethan, do you think we shall have any last days?

MR. N. No; we are but just beginning our existence in this mundane world. Then, Polly, be mine forever. Youth is before us, and heaven near. Girl of my heart, let us cross the threshold together.

MRS. B. Take my hand, Ethan, and be it as you say. The dove moans no longer.   [*Curtain falls.*

AM I ONE?

Characters :

MRS. DOW, *a Widow.*
PETER *and* ROBERT, *her Sons.*
ALICE DOW, *her Niece.*

CHARLES CAREY.
GRACE BARTON.
MR. PENDER.

MRS. DOW, sitting alone upon the stage, dressed in black, with an open book in her hand.

MRS. DOW. 'T is three long years since I have been a heart - broken mourner. 'T is five since my husband died. I sorrowed then, but not without hope ; tears fell, but there was no bitterness in them ; I was lonely, but there was peace in the loneliness. I knew that my good man was in the blessed home prepared for him, and I knew he would wait at the gate for his Mary. But when my darling Robbie took himself from me in that dark night, my heart broke. It will not be comforted. 'T is of no use for Mr. Pender to speak to me kind words ; I cannot listen to him. 'T is of no use for him to talk to me of love and youth. My heart is broken, and I will wear this black crape as the symbol of my grief until I cross the shining river.

(*Enter* MR. PENDER ; *shakes hands with* MRS. DOW.)

MR. PENDER. Still in your dark weeds. Why will you cherish grief ?

Mrs. D. 'T is the all of my life ; leave me in it ; I would have nothing else. Mr. Pender, you speak kindly words, but kindness oppresses me now. My boy Robbie is lost—lost for this world and the other. His mother's heart is broken. How gladly would she die for him!

Mr. P. Since you cannot do this, why not make a sensible woman of yourself, and live for one who would gladly fill Robbie's place ?

Mrs. D. Mr. Pender, your words are powerless. No, not so,—for they give pain. I have grown old in grief. A mother's heart, all unsatisfied, is consuming me.

Mr. P. Since I cannot serve you in one way, command me in any other. What can I do for you ?

Mrs. D. Bring back my lost boy.

Mr. P. Give me a pledge from your finger, and I will search heaven and earth to find him. (*She gives her ring.*) You will see me no more till I bring to your arms your truant child. [*Exit.*

Mrs. D. He is a good man—may the Lord help him in his search! But I have no hope ; my heart is broken ; I can only wait and weep. But Gracie's letters are some comfort. (*Takes a letter from her pocket, and reads.*)

" Do not yield to despair, my dear friend. Hope on, and trust ever. Our dear Robbie will return to us endeared a thousand - fold by his long absence."

Blessed child! If I could only see her. But her father, as if he were afraid my presence would contaminate her, took her away the same week I lost my boy. But I have her weekly letters. She was young when Robbie gave her that lock of hair, with the charge not to forget. And she does not forget; she loves my boy, and her love, buoyant with hope and cheerful with trust, may prove the magnetic star to light his wandering feet home. His mother's love is an agony of despair; it cannot help him; it only makes his way dark and troubled. But dear Gracie! Her love is lighted with hope, and strong with trust. Robbie, my boy, do you not feel the charm? Come home.

(*Enter* ALICE DOW.)

ALICE. Dear Auntie! always sad. Why will you not be a little cheerful for my sake? and more so for poor Peter. He says, since Robbie went away, you take no notice of him; that his home is so gloomy he does n't like to stay under its roof.

MRS. D. I suppose it is; and he is over at your house almost every evening. I trust you to make him happy. I never loved him as I did Robbie; he is cold and taciturn. Robbie was so affectionate and social.

ALICE. But Peter is good; he never ran away; he is always true and kind.

MRS. D. Yes, that is my Peter—true and kind. The sun is true and kind in its wintry light; it never ceases its shining; but who grows warm in its heartless beams? Peter is cold, selfish. Forgive me, my son; you are kind to your mother in your way—but you are *Peter*. The boy of my heart, my wild summer boy, my pet lamb, is wandering in a strange fold. O Good Shepherd! bring him home.

ALICE. Auntie, if you trusted that Good Shepherd you would not feel the lonely wretchedness you do.

MRS. D. That is a merited rebuke, Alice. I accept it kindly. But when Peter tells me there is no use in fretting for Robbie; that he has shown himself a bad boy, and do n't deserve my love, I feel like a swelling volcano, ready to send forth fire and smoke. O, Peter's cold philosophy chills me; he knows nothing of *love*. Robbie, my darling, are you not cold and hungry in that far-off fold?

ALICE. Auntie, do try to leave him with the Good Shepherd that guardeth every fold.

MRS. D. I do leave him there; I must leave him there. But this leaving does not help the heart's agony.

ALICE. Perhaps you do not leave him in the right way.

MRS. D. Alice, your words probe deeply; I do not think I leave him at all. How can I? He is a part of my being. Robbie, come home!

ALICE. Aunt Mary, I had a letter from Gracie yesterday, and I came round here to tell you what she says. She is going to visit me next week. She wants to talk with you about a plan her father has for her. I do n't know what it is, but I think it is something that troubles her.

MRS. D. The cold, hard-hearted man is trying to make her forget Robbie, I know.

ALICE. He has always done this, and I do not know as we ought to blame him. Gracie is his only child, and he loves her dearly. When Robbie was at home, you know he was wild and reckless. Do n't you remember how he coaxed Gracie up on to that high scaffold? She was dizzy, and came near falling and breaking her neck. There was no way for her to get down but to fall into his arms. Cousin Robbie was a rogue. He use to race his horses when Gracie rode with him, to test her courage.. We ought not to blame Mr. Barton very much if he does try to have her forget.

Mrs. D. I do blame him. Robbie liked fun, but he was a good, generous-hearted boy, and so kind and loving.

Alice. It was not very kind in him to run away and break his mother's heart.

Mrs. D. He did not mean it. He could never bear to see his mother suffer. Come home, dear boy ! Mr. Pender thinks he can find him.

Alice. Yes, I met him on the way here. He says he will search heaven and earth, but he will find Robbie. Auntie, why do n't you try to be more cheerful, and leave off this mourning dress? I think Mr. Pender could see better to find the runaway if you did n't look so dark.

Mrs. D. I can 't help his eyes until he brings me Robbie.

Alice. Have you promised him a reward if he does, Auntie? I guessed as much, he is so determined.

Mrs. D. All that I have—all that I am—I will give the man that brings me my boy.

Alice. *Uncle* Pender! I only anticipate the day. I know he will win the prize. He will not sleep until he does.

[*Enter* Peter.]

PETER. Mother, what is the scapegrace up to now? I see in the morning paper there is five thousand dollars reward offered to any person that will give information concerning Rob. This card is to be copied into every paper in the United States and California. What is the harum-scarum boy doing now, that such a reward is offered for his head? I will never give my hard-earned money to save him from prison if he merits it.

MRS. D. Hush, Peter! Smother your chilling thoughts. Have you no heart?

PETER. I have heart enough, but I will not let it make a fool of me. But what do you suppose this great sum of money is offered for? Rob's height, form, and face are all minutely described. Has he been up to some deviltry? What does it mean?

MRS. D. It means, your mother has a friend more thoughtful of her comfort than you are, Peter.

PETER. Gracie has no five thousand dollars to give. If Rob is n't a fool, he will come home and claim the reward himself. But he may not dare to come — he was always full of mischief.

ALICE. Cousin Peter, you are rocky; what makes you so hard? You have a heart?

PETER. Yes; but it is made of flint.

ALICE. And flint strikes fire, but it takes a skilful hand to do it. Fanny Earl knows the art. Now, do n't droop your head, Pete.

PETER. But what does this mean about Rob?

ALICE. Do n't be alarmed. There are more magic hands in the world than Fanny's. I hope the generous reward will bring Robbie from his hiding place. I would

give all I am worth to see him.   Let 's go and read the
advertisement.   [*Exeunt.*

SCENE SECOND.

CHARLES CAREY.   GRACE BARTON.

GRACE.   I did n't expect to meet you here, Mr.
Carey ; I came expecting other friends.

MR. CAREY.   I trust my presence is not disagreeable.
I have sought a long time an opportunity of seeing you
a few minutes alone, but you seem to shun me.

GRACE.   I have a reason for it.

MR. C.   Not a good one.   You have acknowledged
to your father that my character is unexceptionable ;
that you have been very happy in my society ; that you
have seen few persons that you enjoy more.   Then why
should you shun me ?

GRACE.   Mr. Carey, please do n't press me to answer
your question.   Did you enjoy the concert last evening?

MR. C.   No.   I heard as one that did not hear.   I
saw you there with our mutual friend, Mr. James.

GRACE.   Mr. James said the music was fine ; you
know I do not profess to be a judge in that department.

MR. C.   I wish you did not in some others of more
importance.   Gracie, you are a mystery that I cannot
solve.   You are not handsome.

GRACE.   I know it ; but you are, Mr. Carey.

MR. C.   That is my misfortune.   A handsome gentleman is not acceptable to homely ladies ; they prefer
roughs and Shallows.   But you have a cross eye.

GRACE. That depends upon the company I am in. I can look straight if I choose.

MR. C. If you will look straight at me for a moment, perhaps I can read you.

GRACIE. I will not.

MR. C. Please do, and I will grant you any request you may make.

GRACE. Will you cease persecuting me?

MR. C. O Gracie (pardon me), Miss Barton, do not call my devotion to you persecution. Why do you persist in treating me thus? To be rejected by a plain, uneducated mechanic's daughter does not humble me — it almost maddens me. It maddens me to see you make such a fool of yourself. Have you no sense?

GRACE. Sense enough to know when I am in the presence of a gentleman.

MR. C. That is an assumption, but I will grant it, if you will answer me one direct question. Have you a heart of your own?

GRACE. I have not yours, and you deceive yourself if you think I have. Educated gentlemen are sometimes ignorant upon certain very nice subjects.

MR. C. Will your wisdom please enlighten one of them?

GRACE. Love is Heaven's most sensitive flower, and only blossoms in freedom. It *feels*, but does not speak.

MR. C. Then I must love you in silence.

GRACE. You do not love me at all. You are a fashionably educated gentleman; you are a master of many languages; master of the natural sciences; understand all the quibbles of law; you can plead as eloquently for the wrong as for the right; you can talk about love and devotion, ——

MR. C.   Go on, Miss Barton; your enthusiasm makes you almost handsome; your cross-eye becomes fixed; speak on.

GRACE.   You can use hard, rough words to a lady. You can stoop to ridicule and sarcasm to gain a point.

MR. C.   Indeed I would to gain the heart and hand of Gracie Barton. Teach me my lesson: I will be an an apt learner.

GRACE.   Go home, then, and unlearn the many falses that you have learned. Be a true, and sincere, and gentle, man. Mr. Carey, give me the hand of friendship; do not let us talk of love; it *will* not be talked of; it must be *felt*. You do not love me; I cannot love you. We can interest each other; you can teach, and I can learn; but you do not know what love is. In this I am your superior; in nothing else. Now let us be friends.

MR. C.   Tell me first, Gracie, and tell me truly, do you love another?

GRACE.   No gentleman but yourself has ever talked to me of love. Three years ago, a wild, warm-hearted boy gave me a lock of hair—he looked straight into my cross-eye until it became fixed—he only said, "Gracie, don't forget." This is all, Mr. Carey. I cannot forget. Please don't ask me any questions: let us be friends.

MR. C.   Will you not tell me the name?

GRACE.   Do not ask me. Do not speak of this. Father thinks I have forgotten; keep my secret; give me your promise.

MR. C. I wish I were the wild, warm-hearted boy; but you have my promise.

GRACE. Thank you, Mr. Carey. Now let us be friends.

MR. C. As you say.

[*They take hands. The curtain falls.*

SCENE THIRD.

ROBERT Dow alone, walking the stage with an open letter in his hand.

ROB. Am I one? or am I two? I am a mystery to myself. After three years' lonely and painful wandering, I stand again in my native village, have walked beneath the elms that shaded my childhood, have seen the vine-covered cottage—— Beating heart, be still! Am I one? or am I two? Conflicting emotions tear me. Mother, dearest mother, the boy—your wayward pet—is at your feet. " Forgive, forgive!" he cries. Down, down, distracting thought! *Does she live? Hath grief killed her?* Am I one? A devil, an angel, both are in this bosom. Fight on, fight for victory, good angel; the Lord is on your side; He proclaimeth peace when the battle is won. Fight on to the last—yield not an inch of ground till a oneness is complete. (*Looks at the open letter in his hand.*) This will not do. I must nerve myself for the meeting. (*He reads.*) " Five thousand dollars if the information is satisfactory." I can make it satisfactory. I can tell him where he may find Robert Dow. But I must be prudent; must learn why such a sum of money is offered for a runaway.

Possibly some villain wants to lay his burden upon my back ; but I do not believe this. I have faith in human nature ; and this means that I have faith in the good and the true. The devil shall be slain and the oneness come. But if a brother seeks my life, I forgive him as I hope to be forgiven. (*Looks at his watch.*) The hour is here. Mr. Pender, I am ready to see you ; but I must be prudent ; I have money enough in my pocket to take me back to my far-off hiding-place. Mother, dear mother, if she lives, come what will, I am her boy.

[*Enter* MR. PENDER.]

MR. PENDER. (*Bows politely.*) Do I meet Mr. Bush?

ROB. I answer to that name.

MR. P. Then we will proceed to business. Can you give me the whereabouts of Robert Dow ?

ROB. I can.

MR. P. Can you guide me to his place of residence?

ROB. I can.

MR. P. This is sufficient. When you have done it, the promised reward is yours.

ROB. This may be sufficient for you but not for me. I am too much interested in the safety of Robert Dow to betray his hiding-place until I know why so large a sum of money is offered for him.

MR. P. Has the young man committed a crime, that he fears to reveal himself?

ROB. Guard your language, stranger ! Impute not a shadow of crime to the son of Mrs. James Dow.

MR. P. I do not. I reverence and respect that suffering lady too much to question the honor of her son.

ROB. Does she live ?

MR. P. If the anguish of a mother's despair may be called life, Mrs. Dow lives.

ROB. (*walks across the stage, and in low tones says,* Thank God for this.) Mr. Pender, please tell me in few words why this sum of money has been offered for the discovery of Rob. Dow. I know him well, and can take you to him ; but first answer me this question.

MR. P. Sympathy for his suffering mother has prompted it.

ROB. Is the mother still a widow ?

MR. A. She clings to the black veil until she finds her lost boy. It is for him she mourns.

ROB. Has she not another son ?

MR. P. Yes — Peter; but he is little comfort to her since Rob ran away.

ROB. Is not this son kind to her ?

MR. P. Peter is kind to her in his stony way ; but Mrs. Dow refuses all kindness, all comfort, until her lost boy comes home. So show me where he is, and the reward is ready for you.

ROB. What assurance have I of this ?

MR. P. I will deposit a check of five thousand dollars in the hand of a third person.

ROB. Very well ; let the thing be done.

MR. P. Excuse me a moment. If you have no objections, I will now present the brother and mother, with two young lady friends.

ROB. As you please. (*Exit* MR. PENDER) My mother ! She cannot know me. I was a boy when I left her ; I had a boy's slender form, a boy's soft face ; now I am stout and heavy ; my face is browned with the tropical sun and covered with a man's moustache: my hair is long and uncombed; it has grown curly, too, in the southern breezes. Mother will not see her wild boy in the thinking man. My voice—her quick ear will detect that—I cannot change it. I must keep silent. She must not know me yet; I am not prepared. I would meet her alone. And Pete is to be with her; that is well. His cold eye will not know me. The two young ladies—who may they be? One is Cousin Alice, and the other —— Be still, bounding heart! Little Cross-eye could not remember the wayward boy so long.

[*Enter* Mrs. Dow, Peter, Cousin Alice, Grace Barton *and* Mr. Pender.]

Robert. (*Takes from his pocket a pencil and paper and quickly writes.*) To-morrow evening I will make the revelation. (*He gives the paper to* Mr. Pender, *who reads it aloud.*)

Mrs. D. Stranger, gentleman, do not keep us in this terrible suspense. Speak now. Give us your secret. 'T is a mother's aching heart that pleads with you.

Rob. (*In choking voice.*) Madam, will you raise your veil?

(Grace *is faint and sinks into a chair.* Alice *fans her.*)

Mrs. D. I will never raise this black veil from my face until my wandering boy comes home. These eyes of mine shall never see sunlight again until they look upon Robbie. Robbie, my boy.— Robbie, your mother's heart is broken. Come home! come home!

GRACE (*rises slowly, gently takes* MRS. DOW'S *hand, places it to her lips, then raising her veil, says*) Robbie is here !

ROBBIE *falls on his knees before his mother.*

[*The curtain falls.*

THE BIRCH.

Characters:

Mrs. Crossbar.
Nicodemus, *her Son.*
Mr. Solomon Candid.
Hosea Goodnow, *his Nephew.*

Mr. Carlos Bumper, *Phrenologist.*
Pat Riley, *Waiter.*
Joel Tarbox, *Sheriff.*

Mrs. Crossbar, with a large hickory stick in her hand, looking about the stage.

Mrs. Crossbar. Strange what has become of Nick. He 'll catch it when I find him. Should n't wonder if I break that boy's temper; I 've been at him these twelve years. I began on him when he was six months old; have n't forgot his sticking up his back in the cradle. Did n't he feel my flat hand that day? Wal, I ha n't spared the rod; I ha n't spiled my boy that way. But he 'll get lots more afore he 's broke. This is the biggest birch I ever found. (*Looking at it with satisfaction.*) Won't he get it! There 's a pleasure breking a boy in, though sometimes 't is hard work. Nick is getting strong.

[*Enter* Mr. Candid.]

Mr. Solomon, have you seen my boy, Nick anywhere? I have got a job on hand to do for him, and my fingers

132

ache to get hold of the work. I 'll do it up handsomely, won't I ?

MR. CANDID. I have n't seen your son anywhere ; but what has happened ?

MRS. C. You know I 'm his ma. His pa — well, I don't know whatever became of his pa — but he left the headstrong vagabond to my care, and I am bringing him up straight. Solomon was a wise man, and you know he said, " Spare the rod and spile the boy." I do n't mean to be guilty of spiling Nick. Won't I give it to him when I get hold of him ?

MR. C. Solomon's proverb is greatly abused. I would repeat the words to you that our Saviour spake unto Peter : " Put up again thy sword into his place."

MRS. C. Not until I have staggered the devil in Nick. I 'm his ma.

MR. C. Do you love your son ?

MRS. C. 'Twon't do to stop to think about love ; we must use the rod or spile the boy, and I do n't mean to spile mine for the want of a little hot mustard.

MR. C. I have six boys, and I never had a birch in my house ; my boys never disobey me ; they give me no trouble.

MRS. C. I guess they have got a good ma.

MR. C. You have guessed right there — they have a good ma. *She* often stops to *think* how much she *loves* them.

MRS C. And I 'll bet she birches them when their pa is out. To live in the house with six boys and never birch them ! ! ! I 'd like to see the woman that could do it.

Mr. C. Call round and talk with my wife; she will be happy to give you her secret. Perhaps it would help you in the management of your son.

Mrs. C. I want no help, and I want no advice. I should like a little more strength in my arm, and I should like to be a little spryer in finding the sly fox; he is getting more cunning every day, but his ma is able to settle up accounts yet. I always put on till he begs like a drowning man. Well, there is some satisfaction in it, when one's temper is up to the biling pint.

Mr. C. Mrs. Crossbar, I hope you will not be able to find your son; you are ruining him. You are unworthy the name of *mother*.

Mrs. C. And you are unworthy the name you bear, Mr. Solomon. How did you get it? *You* called *Solomon*, and yet you would spare the rod and spile the boy! Good bye to you.   [*Exit.*

Mr. C. I believe there never was a proverb so much abused as this one of Solomon's. How many selfish, ungovernable parents apply it as a soothing syrup to a sensitive conscience. After passion has subsided they are painfully aware of having abused power; then they seek relief in Solomon's soothing syrup. I would like to teach these parents to apply the rod to their own tempers first, then they may be wise to train the immortal germs entrusted to their care.

[*Enter* Nicodemus, *in tattered clothes.*]

Nic. Please, sir, have you seen my mother anywhere?

Mr. C. Why do you seek your mother?

Nic. And I do n't seek her. I would sooner seek a

hungry tiger. I am hiding myself from her. Please, have you seen her?

MR. C. Who is your mother?

NIC. She is Mrs. Crossbar. She carries a big hickory stick in her hand. She goes out washing when she is 'nt birching me.

MR. C. What does she birch you for?

NIC. That is more than I can tell. Sometimes I know; sometimes I do n't. It comes all the same.

MR. C. Do you love your mother?

NIC. What should I love her for? I would sooner now meet a drove of wild cats than meet that fierce woman. But tell me, sir, have you seen her?

MR. C. She was here a moment since, inquiring for you. (NIC. *starts to run.*) Stop, poor child; I will protect you. There is a law in our country to protect animals from the abuse of man. I feel a law in my heart to protect a weak child against the abuse of a woman—I will not say *mother*. The word is too sacred to be applied to this being.

NIC. I tremble; I think she is close here. Sometimes she seems to spring up out of the ground; I can 't hide from her anywhere. I can 't bear her cudgel now, sir, my back is too sore; feel of the ridges there. (MR. CANDID *feels of the boy's back.*)

MR. C. Barbarous cruelty! And this in a land of civilization! a Christian land? The blood of Abel crieth from the ground; I hear the sad moan. Child, will you leave your mother?

NIC. She is no mother to me—she 's a tiger.

MR. C. Will you put yourself under my protection, and obey me as my boys do?

Nic.   Yes, sir.   Don't you hear that woman coming?

Mr. C.   If she comes here, she shall never strike you again.   I have six boys; they all obey me, and they love me.   I never struck one of them.

Nic.   I should like somebody to love.   I hear her coming.   Save me! save me!   (*Catches hold of* Mr. C.'s *arm.*)

[*Enter* Mrs. Crossbar, *in a rage.*]

Mrs. C.   O, you black rascal! I have found you at last.   You have given me a deal of hunting; that's no matter — your bones can settle for it.   Don't hang like a coward to that gentleman's coat-tail; follow your ma; you know who she is; she understands settling accounts.

Nic.   (*In a loud and terrified voice.*)   I'll never follow you again.   I'd sooner follow a raging lion into its den.

Mrs. C.   (*Walks passionately round the stage.*)   You impudent puppy! this gentleman put courage into you, but I will hound it out.   I know my business — I've had practice.

Mr. C.   Mrs. Crossbar, I have taken this helpless child, with his lacerated back, under my protection.   I had six boys this morning; I have seven now.   They are all *my lambs*.   I am their shepherd, and I will guard my *whole* flock.   No dog shall touch the back of one of them.

Mrs. C.   Scoundrel! thief! robber!   Who are *you*, Solomon Candid, that dares rob a woman of her child?   But you can't do it.   You could as easily take a cub from the mouth of a bear, as to take that child from me.

Give me my own, or I 'll birch your six saplings till they can 't stand on their feet. I 'll do for them the work their ma is too cowardly to do.

MR. C. (*Rings a bell. Enter* PAT RILEY.) Patrick, step across the street and order the sheriff over here.

PAT. Yes, sir ; I 'll do it. [*Exit* PAT.

MR. C. Woman, I see you are an unsafe person to run at large — my lambs would be in danger.

[*Enter* SHERIFF.]

Sheriff take this woman into safe custody ; let her wait her trial ; I will appear as witness against her being a safe person to walk the street.

SHERIFF. Woman, follow me.

MRS. C. I never followed a man yet, and I do n't think I shall begin now.

SHERIFF. I am an officer of the city, and must do my duty. If you refuse to follow, I have brother officers within call, and I have handcuffs in my pocket.

MRS. C. I vow vengeance on that black robber there and his six cubs ; they shall become acquainted with Crossbar. The good old proverb shall not be trampled under foot, with no one to defend it, while I live. I 'll have my own. (*She shakes her fist at* MR. CANDID.) I 'll fix him so he 'll never get me into a scrape like this again — the cowardly puppy.

SHERIFF. Come along.

MRS. C. I never followed Crossbar, and I 'll not follow you. Go, give your orders to your own slave wife.

(SHERIFF *rings the bell.* MRS. C. *runs off the stage, and* SHERIFF *follows her.*)

[*Enter* Mr. Bumper.]

Mr. Bumper.   Good evening, Mr. Candid.   I have
brought you a ticket of admission to my lecture this
evening.   Is phrenology popular in this place ?

Mr. C.   People here are somewhat awake to an interest in it.   I think you will have a good house.   Put
your hand on the head of this boy, and tell me what
you think of him.

Mr. B. (*feels of* Nick's *head.*)   This is a remarkable
head.   Boy, you will make something in life ; you will
make a mark ; and much will depend upon surrounding
influences whether the mark is good or bad.   I find
here large combativeness, large destructiveness, and
very large casualty.   His moral qualities are all full, his
self-esteem is large ; he would not very quietly bear
an insult ; he would not patiently bear oppression ; he
is very conscientious ; has a great sense of justice.   He
would make a good soldier, give him the right side to
fight on.

Mr. C.   You think he has a good head, and ought
to be a good boy ?

Mr. B.   He has a fine head ; his firmness is small ;
he wants a kind friend to stand by him, to steady him
a little.   Boy, what is your name ?

Nic.   Nicodemus Crossbar.

Mr. B.   Well, I will give you a word of advice —
set your mark high.   Never do a mean thing ; never
speak a falsehood ; and never *act* one either.   Be faithful in the discharge of everything you undertake to do.
You have the capacity to fill honorably a high position ;
but you have seen trouble.   Can I do anything for you ?

Nic. Yes, sir.

Mr. B. What are you in want of?

Nic. A friend — somebody to trust — somebody to love.

(*He sinks down upon the carpet, and covers his face with his hands. Mr. Candid kindly helps him up, and seats him in a chair.*)

Mr. C. What is the matter with you, Nick?

Nic. (*Places his hand on his stomach.*) I am very tired. It aches, here.

Mr. C. Have you had any supper?

Nic. No, sir.

Mr. C. Did you have any dinner?

Nic. No, sir.

Mr. C. And your breakfast?

Nic. I had my breakfast yesterday morning; since then I have heen all the time hiding; and the longer I hide the more am I afraid of that woman.

Mr. C. Where did you sleep last night?

Nic. I didn't sleep anywhere; I hid myself in a barrel.

[Mr. Candid *rings the bell. Enter Waiter.*]

Mr. C. Pat, give this boy a supper; give him a good one. He's my boy; I'll pay the bill.

Nic. Isn't the woman out there?

Mr. Pat, what became of that woman that was here?

Pat. She ran into the street, and the sheriff after her.

Mr. C. You are safe, Nick; she shall never lay her hands on you again. You are my boy, my seventh son; I will take care of you. Go with Pat.

[*Exeunt* Pat *and* Nic.

Mr. B.   That boy has a remarkable head ; I would like to watch its development.   With a kindly training he will make a reformer — a philanthropist.   But great suffering is written on his face.   I am in haste now. When I am at leisure, I would like to know his history. I can help him, and would like to, — that is, if he is in need of a friend.

Mr. C.   I would like to talk with you about his capacity or fitness for some particular niche in life.   I am much interested in him, and have told him he was my boy.   I will stand by him.

Mr. B.   That is right.   Good evening.   I am in haste.   [*Exit.*

[*Enter* Hosea Goodnow.]

Hosea.   Uncle Solomon, father sent me round to ask you if you could send him a good honest boy, to open his shop mornings, and sometimes carry bundles ?

Mr. C.   I think I can, Hosea.   I have an honest boy on my hands now that I want to get a good place for. I want to put him where he will be treated very kindly. I do not care about any compensation : I will see to that part.   I want this boy to have a genial home.

Hosea.   If he is a good, neat boy, father will take him into our family ; and ma, you know, makes a warm home for everybody under her care.

Mr. C.   Tell your father I will see him in the morning.   I have a boy for him.   'T will be just the place for poor suffering Nick.   Hosea, you are a kind-hearted boy, and your little sister is a bright ray of sunshine. All is right.   [*Exit* Hosea.

[*Enter* Nicodemus.]

Well, Nicodemus, have you had a good supper ?

Nic. Yes, sir, thank you ; I feel better.

Mr. C. I will take you to the tailor's, and then you shall go home with me and pass the night. In the morning, after you are rested, we will talk of your future. That woman shall never strike you again. You shall never sleep in a barrel again. I am your friend. I will stand by you as a father. All that I ask in return is, that you will try to be a good boy.

Nic. I will be a good boy. I have always said, give me a chance and I would be a good boy.

(*Enter* Mrs. Crossbar, *hair flying, looking wild and furious. She grabs* Nick. *Two sheriffs follow with handcuffs.*)

[*Curtain falls.*

THE GOLD SNUFF-BOX.

Characters:

JAMES LIGHTHEART, BETTY RIDECAP,
DAVID GOODYEAR, POLLY DWIGHT.

JAMES (*alone, feels of his head and limbs*). Well, I
do n't know who I am. There has a wonderful change
come over me since yesterday. Yesterday I was a brave
boy — but not now. To-day, I am a coward — I am
afraid of a shadow — I tremble at the rustle of a leaf —
I start at the slightest creaking of the door. [*Enter
DAVID — he starts.*] How you frightened me!

DAVID. I see I did. You used to be a brave boy.
What has happened to you that you are afraid of your
old friend? Have I changed into a bugbear?

JAMES. No, you are not changed. The change is
in me. In one night's time, I have become a coward.
I confess it with shame.

DAVID. What are you afraid of? Has some big
bully whipped you?

JAMES. No; I was never whipped in my life, and
I 'm not afraid of it.

DAVID. Will you fight? It might revive your
courage. You were once brave.

JAMES. I was never afraid until last night. I quiver and shiver now when I think of it. (DAVID *accidentally lets a book fall. JAMES starts.*)

DAVID. Well, something has had hold of you, that is certain. The simple falling of a book makes you start like some old, nervous woman. Let us have a good fight, and that will make a man of you again.

JAMES. I never fight, as you know, David. I never could see use or fun in it. But I was never a coward until now.

DAVID. That is true. Everybody that knows James Lightheart, knows he is a brave boy. We have all seen his courage. When every other boy ran, he stayed to save a child from the bite of a mad dog; and he came near being drowned once, in doing a kindness for Miss Ridecap. (JAMES *starts.*) Well, what is the matter with you? Are you sick? You look pale.

JAMES. I am not sick, unless I am sick at heart.

DAVID. But what made you start just now. There is nothing here, and I did n't drop a book.

JAMES. I am fearfully changed. The simple mention of a person's name startles me.

DAVID. Unburden your soul, Jim · make a clear confession — I will keep it safe.

JAMES. Do you know this, David? (*He takes a golden snuff-box from his pocket.*)

DAVID (*looks at it*). No, I 'm sure I do n't.

JAMES. Well, 't is this golden snuff-box that has metamorphised me. You have volunteered to be my confessor; now listen to my story, and keep it safe.

DAVID. I give you my word for it.

JAMES.   Just one year ago yesterday, I found Uncle Joe's pocket-book in our garden.   It contained a thousand dollars.   You know he lives three good miles from here.   I showed mother what I had found, and asked her if I might eat my supper before I took it round to Uncle Joe.   She said "yes."   'T was a cold night — I shall never forget it.   I had a long walk.   When I went into Uncle Joe's room, he was walking the floor, looking anxious and pale.   I gave him the pocket-book. He grabbed it as a starving dog would a bone.   After looking to see if the money was safe, he said, "Where and when did you find this?"   I answered, "in the garden, at four o'clock this afternoon."   Now, David, what do you suppose he gave me for my honesty and my long tramp?

DAVID.   Half there was in the pocket-book.

JAMES.   He gave me a hard scolding; called me a lazy blockhead for eating my supper before I ran to him with the pocket-book.   When I got home that night, with aching fingers and weary limbs, I said to myself, the time-honored adage, "Honesty is the best policy," will not stand a test.

DAVID.   And that was a hard lesson; but it happened a year ago.   What has it to do with the coward of to-day, and the snuff-box?

JAMES.   It has much to do with it — everything. 'T is the cause of all my suffering last night.   If I should go to State's prison, Uncle Joe will be very much to blame.

DAVID.   Explain yourself, Jim; don't keep me in this terrible suspense.   I shall soon be trembling.   I'm ready for a start now. What of State's prison? (*A window falls.* JAMES *tries to hide himself.*) James, do speak out. What is the matter?

JAMES. Well, I feel like somebody beside myself. Am I Jim Lightheart? Do you know me, David?

DAVID. No, I do n't know you. Please introduce yourself.

JAMES. I am the mean, wicked boy that found Betty Ridecap's golden snuff-box last night.

DAVID. Well, if you know it is hers, why do n't you return it to her?

JAMES. This is just what I have concluded to do, as soon as I come fairly to my senses.

DAVID. Why did n't you return it last night?

JAMES. That's a pointed question, David. I have learned two lessons within the year. Uncle Joe taught me to disrespect the old adage — I just despised it; and when I found Miss Betty's snuff-box of gold, I said to myself, Jim Lightheart knows a better policy than honesty, and I put the found treasure into my pocket, and walked leisurely home. I had no appetite for my supper. I did not enjoy my mother's company, so I seated myself on the door-sill, to watch the coming of the stars; but I soon forgot to look at them. I began thinking. The night grew dark, and my thoughts grew darker. Puss came, in her usual friendly way, and rubbed against me; I screamed, but on finding it was Pussy, I took her into my lap, and kept her for company. Next, I felt a hard blow on my forehead; this frightened me terribly, and I ran into the house. O, David, how changed I am!

DAVID. I should think so. But what struck you on your forehead?

JAMES. I thought at the time that all the powers of darkness had consolidated themselves into a fist of iron; but since reason has begun to return, I think it was a bat. You know they are birds of the night, and I suppose they thought I was one of them, and what I took to be a blow on my forehead, was intended only as a recognition — perhaps an introduction — into their society.

DAVID. I am glad to see a little fun left in you, Jim; 't is a good symptom — Lightheart will triumph yet.

JAMES. I begin to think he will, since I have spoken to you about this hellish affair. I am using strong terms, David, but it 's all from hell, and smells of brimstone. I begin to feel better — light dawns. I know what I shall do before I sleep another night. O, last night! 'T was awful; full of hobgoblins.

DAVID. How did your hobgoblins look, Jim?

JAMES. Do n't make fun of it, David. I shiver now, when I think what I saw and felt. In the first place, when I went to bed I had become such a coward I was afraid to blow my light out, so I got into bed with it burning. A long while I laid there, looking steadily at it, hoping in this way to silence thought. 'T was of no use. I had put the snuff-box under my pillow, for safe keeping. When I was just sinking into a sleep, a mouse ran along in the ceiling. I sprang for the snuff-box, screaming, " You shan't have it." This awoke me, and again I fixed my eyes upon the light. And now, without seeming to be asleep, I saw, standing in the corner of my room, a giant. His skin was black, his mouth was open; and such teeth! and such a large throat! O, I shudder to think of the spectre!

DAVID. Well, what did this fine-looking gentleman say to you?

JAMES. He had in his bony hand a large iron rope. He took a step towards me, and began to spit fire. I tried to run, but could not move; then I tried to scream, but could utter no sound. Now, this evil thing made a noose of his iron rope, and threw it towards me, calling out at the same time, " You black thief!"

DAVID. Did this policeman catch you, Jim?

JAMES. No, I was too quick for him. I gave a jump, which awoke me. Now darkness was in the room; my candle had burnt down into the socket. I covered my head with the bed-clothes, to protect it from the fist of iron; and not only this, I was fearful I might see that demon again. I laid awake some hours, then fell into another fearful sleep. Now, I was in terrible cutting pain — I writhed in agony. When I tried to call mother, I saw a doctor standing beside my bed. His nose was so long it almost touched my face; his eyes were like two balls of fire; he held a long tube in his hand, and made me open my mouth; then he put the tube into it, and began blowing snuff down my throat; and he growled out, " 'T is a case of life or death." I felt as if I was suffocating, and made another jump. This awoke me, and how thankful I was to see the sun shining!

DAVID. Well, Jim, you have been treated very harshly for your folly, and your Uncle Joe is all to blame.

JAMES. I thought so at first, but not now, David. When I carried home Uncle Joe's pocket-book, I did n't see things in a clear light. I had always been taught that "honesty is the *best* policy." You know this time-honored adage, in some hidden way, conveys to the mind an idea of a reward. Still, I do n't know as I expected anything from my uncle. If he had spoken kindly to me, and then thanked me, I believe I should have felt satisfied. It was his rough manner and his ingratitude that wrought the mischief.

DAVID. Your Uncle Joe was very much to blame. Ingratitude is a crime almost as great as dishonesty. I do n't forgive him; he has caused you all this trouble.

JAMES. Not exactly, David. I do n't think my uncle acted the part of a Christian gentleman, in his rude manner; but, then, in the end it may do me good. It led me to do a wicked act, which has brought, as a consequence, much fear and suffering, and this fear and suffering has led to much thinking; and I believe I have thought things clear. This time-honored adage will not bear the light of these latter days. One word must be changed. Instead of *best*, read *only*, and you will see a saving difference. "Honesty is the only policy."

DAVID. Well, Jim, that little change does make a difference — honesty is the *only* policy. This pins it tight. Let Uncle Joe bluster as much as he pleases, there is no driving an honest boy from the track with this adage in his head.

JAMES. So you see, David, Uncle Joe was not the only cause of my being hung with an iron rope, and filled with snuff. I was leaning on a faulty adage; but it is righted now. Honesty is the *only* policy, and all the snuff-boxes in creation, tied to all Uncle Joe's scolding, could never tempt me again to sleep over what is not rightfully my own. Now, I will go and carry Miss Betty Ridecap her lost treasure, and then I shall be myself again. Will you go with me, David?

[*Exeunt.*

SCENE SECOND.

[*Enter* BETTY RIDECAP.]

BETTY (*greatly distressed*). Well, this is more than I can bear. I can't be resigned to it any way. When our minister told us the last days were drawing nigh, and urged us so make ourselves ready, he found Betty Ridecap one of the most cheerful and resigned of his people. (I did n't believe all the minister said.) (*Feels in her pocket.*) But this thing I do believe, *my gold snuff-box is gone*, and I am just distracted. I will never take another pinch of snuff, until I find my box. 'T was my great-gran'ther's — 't was a family relic. I can't bear the loss. I can't bear such trouble now; my hair already shows the touch of winter's frosty fingers, and one night more of such suffering as I had last night, and my head is as white as chalk. But I do n't care about my white head, nor my suffering, so I can get my box again. I'd give half my farm for it. I am all distracted. I suppose some of them city blacklegs have been round here.

[*Enter* POLLY DWIGHT.]

POLLY. Miss Ridecap, my mother sent me round to invite you over to our house this evening. Mr. Drummond is going to be there, and you understand what that means, without any explanation.

BETTY. Dear, dear me! How opposites do sometimes meet! First a great trouble — almost more than any Christian can bear — then a joyous surprise coming on top of it, is enough to craze one. Polly, I do n't think I can appear to any advantage to-night. It might just upset the whole affair. I am distracted. You see, I am so distracted, I should talk to Mr. Drummond about my snuff-box half the evening. If he should say anything nice to me, I could not answer him becomingly. You see I am just distracted. How do I look?

POLLY. You look distracted. What has happened to you?

BETTY. Well, then, *I do look distracted!* It will not do to see Mr. Drummond in this way. It might upset the whole thing. How many children has he?

POLLY. Six. But what is the matter with you?

BETTY. And how large is his farm?

POLLY. A hundred acres — mortgaged. But what is the matter? What has happened?

BETTY. (*Puts her hand in her pocket.*) It is gone! Do you know anything how soon he wants to be married?

POLLY. Miss Ridecap, I should think you were not only distracted, but crazy — wild. Your eyes look strained out of your head, and your hair — well, it looks as if you had wound it round a distaff, for grandma to

spin into thread. Mr. Drummond has never said that
he wanted to be married at all. He simply said he
would like the opportunity of meeting you, so ma has
invited you round to our house this evening.

BETTY. Well, I do n't believe I had better go.
Tell Mr. Drummond I am engaged at the parson's
to-night. My eyes look too bad, of course. My hair I
could fix — I would n't mind going to the barber's for
that; but the barber, you know, could n't fix my eyes,
and there is no oculist in town. Get me excused; your
ma can manage it for me. Fix upon another evening.
She might say I have fifty-six acres and a half on my
farm, and 't is n't mortgaged. Say it is an heir-loom;
do n't say anything about the snuff-box.

[*Enter* JAMES *and* DAVID.]

JAMES. (*Presenting the snuff-box.*) Miss Ridecap,
I have brought you your gold snuff-box. (*Betty raises
her hands.*) I found it last evening in the woods, half
hid under the leaves. Excuse my not returning it to
you sooner.

BETTY. And that I will, Master James Lightheart.
Heaven be praised, and the earth, and the moon, and
the stars! (Polly, tell your ma I will be round there.)
James Lightheart, I was just saying, I 'd give half my
farm for this same box. (*Takes a pinch of snuff.*) And
I 'll keep my word. Which half will you have?

JAMES. I will not have any of it, and only regret
that I did n't bring the box to you last night.

BETTY. We 'll not talk about that. To be sure I
suffered enough. You know this box was my great-
gran'ther's; I set my life by it. Of course I could n't

sleep, when I did n't know where the precious thing was. If I had knowed it was in your safe keeping, I should have rested easy. Some wicked people would have kept it; I knowed enough of human nater to be aware of this; and I was just distracted. I took my candle-lantern, and raked all over my chip-yard at twelve o'clock last night.

DAVID. Did you think you lost it there?

BETTIE. I knew I did n't lose it there; but one must do something when one is distracted.

JAMES. Miss Ridecap, do you forgive me for keeping it over night?

BETTY. Have n't I said I did? It's an old saying, that an *honest man* is the noblest work of God; and, verily, I believe an *honest boy* is nobler. But, James, I am going to give you something. I have got the best dog in the town, but then he is my guardian; I would not feel safe without him — may-be I shall have a different one, but this is not settled yet. My Maltese cat I think lots of — but then you would n't; she is kind of grown to me. I'll tell you what I'll give you. David may go along with you, and you may take your choice out of my six steers. Will that satisfy you? That white-face one, they say, will make a noble ox.

JAMES. I shall not be satisfied to take anything but your pardon for my delinquency. Honesty is the *only* policy!

BETTY. Well, James Lightheart, we do n't know what may happen. You see my hair is frosty; if I die with my name Betty Ridecap, attend my funeral as first mourner; my will I shall leave in my secretary drawer.

We do n't know what may happen. Should you get an invitation to a wedding, be sure you accept it, and bring David along with you. We do n't know what may happen. Mr. Drummond has three girls and a nice farm. But, James, all these advantages lie in the future; I should feel better to give you something now. What will you have?

JAMES. Your pardon for my remissness. Beside this, I only ask for the brave spirit that honesty always brings. 'T is getting late, I must go. Good evening. (*Shakes hands with Betty.*)

[*Exeunt* JAMES *and* DAVID.

BETTY. Now, Polly, say to your ma I will be round there.

POLLY. Shan't I arrange your hair for you?

BETTY. Not a bit of it. I 'll step into the barber's, and let him touch it up a little with the color of youth. I would n't practise deception, but then it 's right to look as young as you can on an occasion like this. It only comes once is a lifetime. I think I shall look handsome to-night, for I feel so happy — a kind of grateful feeling sets my heart all a-dancing. I have my snuff-box. (*Takes a pinch.*) I should like to sing some of Tom Moore's sentimental poetry, but I have n't time now. Matters press; let us hurry on. [*Exeunt.*

CATNIP TEA.

Characters:

MISS TUBS, *Quack Doctor.*
MISS COB, *Traveling Agent.*
MR. POUND, *an Invalid.*
PETER BURGESS.
DOLLY *and* PHŒBE, *his Sisters.*

LILLIE BURGESS, *his Cousin.*
EMELINE PURINGTON.
SALLY MINT.
ABRAHAM TAYNTOR.

DOLLY and PHŒBE BURGESS, dressed for a dancing party.

DOLLY. I hope we shan't have to wait here very long for Peter; my ears are just aching to hear the thrill of music.

PHŒBE. My feet are aching to move in time to it. I never feel so good as when I am dancing. There is something in music and motion with it that hushes every stormy passion. A man with murder in his heart could n't dance; and if a girl comes on to the floor filled with envy and jealousy, she would, in less than a half hour, have danced it all away. One is in love with everybody when dancing.

DOLLY. This is true, Phœbe. Ma, you know, said, at the supper table to-night, if she felt well enough, she would like to step into the hall for a half hour, if it were only to see the smiling faces there.

154

PHŒBE. I wish she could. All is harmonious in a dance. Music is harmony. Then, motion to it or with it brings us into a complete oneness.

DOLLY. O yes; but there is a prejudice against it in the minds of many, and this arises from so many fast people abusing it. The day is coming when the parlor dance will take the lead in all forms of recreations.

[*Enter* LILLIE.]

LILLIE. Cousins, I have come in to look at you. I like to look at you in your white dresses and flowers. Peter says he will take me with him when I am sixteen years old. I have got to wait four years for that pleasure ; but I do n't think I will stand still all this time. I can hop in the parlor dances, in the school - yard, and in the croquet ground.

PHŒBE. What is Peter doing, Lillie, that he keeps us waiting here so long ? Do you know ?

LILLIE. Yes; he is waiting for Dan to warm the the horses' bits, they are all frost. I think Cousin Peter is a good - hearted fellow ; he says, Old Jack shall not suffer from any impatience of his to get to the dance. I like to see a man take such good care of a horse's mouth. Peter will be blessed for this ; my heart blesses him now.

[*Enter* DR. TUBS, *a large old woman, with saddle bags on her arm.*]

DR. TUBS. I thought I 'd just look, gals, afore you started, to see if you were dressed warm. (*Looks them over.*) Wal, 't will do tolerably well ; 't is n't so much matter about it, seeing I 'm in the house. If anything happens to you in the hall, send the waiter quick for

Dr. Tubs ; I shan't charge you anything for my services, seeing I am boarding with your ma.

[*Enter* PETER.]

PETER. You here, Dr. Tubs? Will you go to the dance with us?

DR. T. I'm a little too heavy for a dance now. I will send these bills instead. Each of you take one. (*Gives them.*) Stick them up in the most sightly place you can find. There is a deal contained in these pieces of paper. But you are in a hurry; go, tell everybody you see that Dr. Tubs's in town, for one week only; say she is the seventh child of a seventh child, and takes docterin' the natral way.

DOLLY. I will remember you; good night.

DR. T. Lillie, child, call your cousins back a moment: I've a word for them.

[LILLIE *calls; they return impatiently.*]

I want to caution Peter about letting you get sweaty. Gals are made of delicate stuff, and must be seen after. When you come home, take a drink of catnip tea; I will leave some standing on the table. Go now, and remember all I've said, particularly about my being the seventh child. Now, Lillie dear, have you any ail about you?

LILLIE. No, ma'am; I'm perfectly well.

DR. T. Come, let me feel your pulse, you may be mistaken. Little gals like you are not very wise; they must be seen after; you do n't get a chance like this every day to be doctored. It will cost you nothing — I shall turn it in for my board.

LILLIE. I am perfectly well, Dr. Tubs; I never felt a pain in my life.

Dr. T. That is no assurance that you never will. Come, let me feel your pulse. (*She counts aloud, one, two, three, up to ten.*) Well, I understand your case ; 't is latent, to be sure ; you are not now suffering, yet the wisest man on earth can 't tell how soon some malignant disease may break out ; and a woman can 't tell either. I 'm a seventh child of a seventh child, and I can 't tell if you will be in health to-morrow. So, you see, it 's best to take precaution. Do n't you sometimes feel a pain in your left side, under the shoulder blade ?

LILLIE. I never felt a pain in my life.

DR. T. That proves, then, what I said — your disease is latent. (*The old woman takes many parcels from her saddle bags and lays them on a table : sits down.*) Now, Lillie, can you remember what I tell you ? Steep this in a quart of soft water, drink a glass of it three times a day, eat such food as you like — let it be cooked ; sleep on a good bed, and get up in the morning when you wake. Can you remember all this ?

LILLIE. I do n't think I shall try very hard. I 'll not take medicine before I 'm sick ; and I doubt if I take much if I am.

DR. T. Well, gals are always foolish ; they need a deal of looking after. I 'll leave this paper with you ; 't won't cost you anything ; I 'll apply it on board.

LILLIE. What kind of medicine do you give, Dr. Tubs ?

DR. T. That 's a pinted question. If I belonged to the faculty, I should n't tell you ; for a good reason, too. Since my art all lies in this, — I 'm the seventh child of a seventh child, I can speak freely. My art,

you see, is patented; no one can copy it, no one can
take it from me. To speak as learned ones speak, no
one can infringe; I am clean above their reach.

LILLIE. Do you give homœopathic remedies?

DR. T. Lar, no, child; there's no power in them
ar little pills. They are not worth the trimming of one
of your finger-nails. My medicine is wonderful; 't is
a great panacea that cures all diseases. It just searches
the system through; it goes into every corner; it
reaches from the worst case of consumption to a wart
on the end of the nose. It cures everything. 'T is just
ruining all life insurance companies.

LILLIE. Do you give mineral medicines, Dr. Tubs?

DR. T. *Mineral medicines! mineral medicines!* I
do n't dabble with those dangerous tools. I 'm the
seventh child of a seventh child — these few words tell
my story.

LILLIE. But you give some medicine?

DR. T. To be sure I do. My medicine is tremendous powerful, and yet it will not harm a cat. Did ever
you know a cat to die before its time came? Cats are
like me — they are born into the laws of life; they
do n't need learning from books. And in one respect
they are like you — their disease is latent. Cats never
suffer pain; and why? Because they are born into the
laws of life; they take medicine before disease comes,
then there is no need of taking it afterwards. Now, if
you will learn wisdom from the seventh son of a seventh
son (excuse me, I did n't mean to say *son*, for I despise
the masculine sex), I would say child, you would take
that parcel of charmed herbs home and drink it, as I

told you. 'T won't cost you anything — I 'll apply it on board.

LILLIE. What is it, Dr. Tubs?

DR. T. You inquisitive little ninny! Are you a seventh son?

LILLIE. I am an only daughter.

DR. T. Then it 's safe to tell you. The wonderful and powerful medicine I use is *Catnip Tea*. 'T will cure every ill flesh is heir to, after passing through my hands. Now take this parcel, and believe what I tell you. [*She takes it and goes.*

[*Enter* MR. POUND, *a large man, on crutches.*]

MR. POUND. Good evening, Dr. Tubs. I have heern of your fame, and have rode ten miles to lay my case before you. I have suffered forty years from the most painful gout. I have spent one farm on the doctors; none of them can help me. I have another farm; I 'm willing to give that if I can purchase youth and health with it.

DR. T. Your case is an awful one, and I 'm glad you heered of me afore it was too late. In the grave you 're past hope; but this side of it there 's life. I 've never seen a case my medicine do n't reach. Cash in hand, I warrant a cure. If the sick want my assistance, they must come quick : I 'm always in a hurry — business presses so, I never stay but a week in a place. I scatter myself as much as possible, that I may do all the good I can. Your disease is of long standing. 'T will cost something to get rid of it; but I can cure it.

MR. P. Thank you for that assurance. I do not

mind expense, so that I can run about again. Forty years of pain makes one hold money lightly.

Dr. T.   I will feel your pulse. (*Hesitates; counts.*) O, they are mighty quick. Do n't wonder you are willing to give a farm just to have them regular. Get them regulated, then all will be regulated. You know, if a watch do n't tick right the time is worth nothing. I have seen many a watch that had the gout — the ticking goes like lightening then. And this is the way your pulse is.

Mr. P.   Give me your wonderful medicine. I 'm impatient to feel this griping, cutting pain let go its awful hold.

Dr. T.   Here are twelve papers of the healing herb; steep one at a time in a quart of soft water; drink of it three times a day. Eat such food as you like — have it cooked; sleep well at night in a warm room; get up in the morning when you feel like it.

Mr. P.   How soon may I begin to walk without these troublesome crutches?

Dr. T.   As soon as your limbs feel like it. When you feel like running and jumping, you may safely do so; it won't harm you.

Mr. P.   I am so thankful to find something at last that will give me back health. A man will give all that he has for health. I have two neighbors that will be coming to you when they see me running about like a boy again.

Dr. T.   They 'd better not wait for that time; I may be in England then. My business is very extensive. If they want to be cured, the sooner they come the better.

Mr. P. I 'll advise them in this direction. If you 'll give me my bill I 'll be getting home, as I have to move slowly.

Dr. T. Do you care to have me write it out ? I 'm not much of a writer.

Mr. P. I do n't want to stop for any writing. What is my bill ?

Dr. T. Seeing you have paid so much for useless doctoring, I will be easy with you.

Mr. P. Thank you for this consideration. My long sickness has drawn heavily on my purse. My wife and children begin to fear the almshouse ; but I encourage them by telling them that is better than the gout.

Dr. T. Well, that is true, and I hope you will suffer neither This medicine will finish up the job, and you can spry about again ; my bill is only fifty dollars.

Mr. P. (*Moves in his chair uneasily.*) That is more money than I have with me. Can you not call it less ?

Dr. T. Seeing you have paid so much to ignoramuses, I will be very easy with you — I will call it forty dollars. That is a small sum to pay for freedom from the gout.

Mr. P. That is true. (*Gives her the money.*)

Dr. T. All right. I shall be glad to see you a boy again. Good night.

Mr. P. Good night. I 'll be glad to feel myself a boy again.   [*Exit* Pound.

[*Enter* Abraham Tayntor.]

Abraham. Is this Dr. Tubs ?

Dr. T. I am the famous Dr. Tubs.

Abraham. One of the young ladies at the dance has

slipped down and sprained her ankle badly. Miss Dolly Burgess sent me to you for something to relieve her.

Dr. T.   Bless Miss Dolly — she is faithful.   I'll remember her in the settlement.   Take this parcel over to the hall, tell the waiter to steep it in a quart of soft water, let the young lady drink of it three times a day, then bathe her sprain in some of it.   Cash in hand, I warrant a cure.

Abraham.   I was not authorized to pay for it.

Dr. T.   My medicine is expensive; I can't afford to give it to strangers.   My advice in this particular case I'll give in.   I'll give it in compliment to Miss Burgess.   I only charge for the medicine ; one dollar.

Abraham.   (*Reluctantly pays the dollar.*)   I don't like this business.   [*Exit.*

Dr. T.   I have lighted on a very good cornfield.   I must pull fast while I'm in here.   'T won't do to stay long.

[*Enter* Emeline Purington.]

Emeline.   Is Dr. Tubs in ?

Dr. T.   I am the person you are in search of.

Em.   I have just read your advertisements all round the town ; I see there is nothing you don't cure.   Do you cure corns ?

Dr. T.   To be sure I do.   Corns are nothing in my diggings.   I can root out the worst of 'em afore you have time to think on 't.

Em.   Do you cure permanently ?

Dr. T.   It's no cure if I don't.   Cash in hand, all cures warranted.

Em.   What do you charge ?

DR. T. My smallest charge, in any case, is one dollar.

EM. That is a big price for curing a corn.

DR. T. Won't you take a dollar's comfort freed from all suffering? What I shall give you will improve your health generally.

EM. Give me the remedy; I won't mind the pr.ce; my corn is very troublesome.

DR. T. Take this parcel, steep it in a quart of soft water, drink of it three times a day; every time you drink of it, bathe your corn with it. You will not feel any change under a week; then your corn will fall out of itself.

EM. (*Pays the dollar.*) Thank you. Good night.

[*Exit.*

DR. T. One dollar is better than nothing.

[*Enter* SALLY MINT.]

SALLY. Am I addressing Dr. Tubs?

DR. T. 'T is the same person you are speaking with.

SALLY. I am suffering terribly with the asthma. Have you anything that will help me?

DR. T. To be sure I have. I have cured persons afflicted with that drawing disease, when their necks were stretched as long as a swan's. Have you had it long?

SALLY. Ever since I was a child. I have to sit up all night — can 't breathe if I lie down.

DR. T. That 's awful. 'T will be an expensive thing to cure, but I can cure it. What can you afford to give to get rid of this life-long ailment?

SALLY. I am not rich, but I 'll pay all I can, so that I may once more breathe easy. What should you charge me?

DR. T. If you were rich, I should charge you forty dollars. If you belong to the middling class, I will cure you for ten dollars. Cash in hand, cure warranted.

SALLY. I do n't belong even to the middling class. I am alone in the world, and poor.

DR. T. In that case, I 'll call it five dollars. I 'm always charitable to the poor.

SALLY. I hav n't five dollars to give you, unless you wait till I earn it.

DR. T. How much have you got that you can pay me?

SALLY. I have only one dollar.

DR. T. Wal, I never turn away a suffering sister because she is poor, if I can help them. Give me your dollar. (*She gives it.*) Now, take this parcel, steep it in a quart of soft water, drink it three times a day. You will not feel any benefit from it the first week; after that you will breathe as freely as a duck in water.

SALLY. I am greatly obliged to you. I think I shall never feel my breath coming easy but I shall remember gratefully Dr. Tubs. [*Exit.*

DR. T. Poor thing! I wish the catnip tea might help her. I hated to take her dollar; but it 's my business. I can 't help it.

[*Enter* MISS COB.]

Madam, take a chair; you look weary.

MISS COB. I am not fatigued at all. (*Opens her large satchel.*) I have many things of interest here. I hardly know what to shew you first. Are you fond of pictures?

DR. T. I 've no liking for pictures.

MISS C. I've a wonderful little machine here for working button - holes.

DR. T. I never have any button - holes; I use hooks and eyes.

MISS C. I have a new kind of hooks and eyes that I would like to show you.

DR. T. I am the famous Dr. Tubs. I do not give my mind to such trifling things as you have. I have a wonderful medicine here; 't is a universal panacea for all the ills that human flesh is heir to. I should judge from your complexion that you had the liver complaint. If you please, I will feel your pulse; I shall make no charge for that.

MISS C. My health is perfectly good. I have lived sixty years; never took any medicine in my life. I never felt a pain.

DR. T. Your case is a remarkable one. When disease takes hold on you it will take hold mighty hard, let me tell you. 'T is in your system now, in a latent form. 'T is an old saying, an ounce of prevention is better than a pound of cure. I will let you have one of my little parcels here that will safely carry you on to the age of ninety in the same state of preservation that you now are in.

MISS C. You say you do n't want anything I have here. Perhaps I can interest you in some other way. I am an agent for a life insurance company. Perhaps you would like to get your life insured.

DR. T. Now that 's ridiculous. My medicine is just ruining all the life insurance companies in the country. Whoever lays in one of my life - giving parcels of medicine is insured. He will live until the last sand has gently run from his glass. I am the seventh child of a seventh child. I see very far into things ; I see your liver is in a torpid state.

MISS C. I 'll take none of your humbug to wake it up ! *[Leaves hastily.*

DR. T. Wal, all agents are sharp. I 've never got one of 'em to take my catnip tea. Wal, I ought not to complain, I am making a mint of money. This catnip tea is a wonderful herb — cats eat it and never die. I 'll be going over to my boarding place now. I must look after the health of that family while I am with them. Peter is a nice-looking boy. If I had n't taken such a dislike to the masculine gender, I should be melted by Peter ; he 's a nice boy. Wal, let gals marry that want to, — I am wedded to Catnip Tea. (*Gathers up her parcels.*)

[*Curtain falls.*]

WHAT MAKES A MAN?

Characters:

FRED BENSON, GEORGE FRANKLIN *and* NED GREENY.

FRED BENSON sits at a table with an arithmetic and slate before him and pencil in his hand.

[*Enter* GEORGE FRANKLIN.]

GEORGE. What have you found, Fred, in that riddle of an arithmetic so interesting?

FRED. 'T is that sum about the geese and half a goose. Now, sit down here, George, and let us get it out together.

GEORGE. Not this moonlight evening, you may be sure of that. I read the sum over, and do not believe there is any " get out " to it; and in the morning, when our lessons come, I am going to guess at the answer. But, away with your book; the boys are all on the common for a game of ball; let us get there to answer to our names when called.

FRED. I cannot go with you, George; father and mother are away at the lecture, and I cannot leave the house.

GEORGE. Did they say you must not leave it?

FRED. They said nothing about it. But what difference does that make, since I know they do not wish me to go?

GEORGE. I think it makes a great deal of difference. You can go out now and not disobey them.

FRED. Do you remember our teacher's dividing boys into three classes, yesterday?

GEORGE. Yes; and what if I do?

FRED. Well, should I go out this evening, knowing it to be wrong, I should sink down into the third class, and I intend to stand always in the first.

GEORGE. I did n't understand the teacher's meaning about the classes, and I wish you did n't.

FRED. Well, I do, and let me explain it to you. He said there were three classes of boys,—the third class could only be governed by threats and the whip; the second class by strong commands given in very forcible language; while it was enough for the first to simply know his duty.

GEORGE. I do not care about these nice distinctions, Fred; they are troublesome.

FRED. Do you not think it much more troublesome to be obliged to listen to threats, commands and hard words? To have some one scream out to you, "*go and do that*, or you will feel my hand on you!" How much there is in the manner a person speaks to you—in the tone of voice. If I were treated in this rough, brutal way, I think I might become a bad boy.

GEORGE. How are you treated?

FRED. I am treated like a person of common sense. I am told in gentle tones what is right to be done, and I try to do it. Now I know what is right to do this evening, and you must not urge me to go out for a game of ball. I am a *boy*.

GEORGE. I supposed so, and that is the very reason that I urge you to a game of ball. Were you a *girl*, instead of asking you to go on to the common I would bring you a wax doll and some sugar plums, and say, " Please stay at home with mamma, while we boys have a good play."

FRED. You do not understand me, George. I am a *boy ;* were I a *dog*, you might *whistle* and I should follow you, right or wrong.

GEORGE. Then come, Fred, be a dog once, and follow me. (*He whistles.*)

FRED. No ; I cannot sacrifice my *boyhood*. I might not find the return to it so easy. Now, my sight is clear — I can always tell the right from the wrong, and so far as I act the right I am becoming a man. If I act the wrong I shall become *less* than a dog, for dogs live according to the light given them.

GEORGE. Where did you get all these thoughts, Fred ? They are quite new to me. I like to take what liberty I can, and never stop to think whether I am a boy, a dog, or a green parrot.

FRED. These thoughts have been coming to me ever since I was lame, three years ago. Then, I had to lie many weeks on the bed, and then I first began to think, and my first subject of thought was *man*.

GEORGE. A game of ball is better than thinking about man. Let us be boys in our young days, and have fun. Do n't let us trouble ourselves about being dogs, baboons, or monkeys.

FRED. I agree with you in this, George; in our young days let us be *boys*, for 't is the *boy* that makes the man. I should like to know something of the early days of our great men. We know George Washington was a good boy; he was remarkable for his truthfulness and industry. And I do not remember reading the life of any of our distinguished men that did not in some way distinguish themselves in boyhood.

GEORGE. There is much truth in that, Fred, I know, for I have read history and biography. But don't you admit that boys need fun?

FRED. Of course I do. And I am not trying to dissuade you from ball playing. I am only excusing myself from the game this evening, because I should not have time to get my lessons in the morning, and it would not be right to leave the house alone.

GEORGE. Just once, Fred, throw aside your scruples.

FRED. *Just once* is what ruins boys. I should like to know what kind of a *boy* Ned Greeny was. He is six feet tall now, but not a *man*. People call him "poor Greeny." They blame him, they pity him, and they make all manner of fun of him. Every improbable story that is told in the neighborhood, they call one of Greeny's stories. He is sick half the time, and the doctor says he has no control of himself—he has either eaten or drank too much. He is a tomfool for everybody. He will believe things exactly opposite each other. You can lead him just as you please. He is like a dog — whistle, and he will follow you. I wish I knew what kind of a boy he was.

[*Enter* GREENY, *with a torn hat and ragged clothes.*]

GREENY. I will tell you ; I will tell you what kind of a boy he was ; yes, I will tell you.

FRED. You have surprised us, Mr. Greeny. We little thought you were near, listening to our conversation.

GREENY. Poor Greeny is always where he should n't be.

FRED. Will you give us the history of your boyhood? I think it must have been remarkable.

GREENY. Yes, it was remarkable ; and that is what makes me a remarkable man. But I heard you say Poor Greeny was not a *man*. You called him a dog. See these two big hands. (*He holds them up.*) They could break your boy bones into atoms.

FRED. I did n't call you a dog, Mr. Greeny ; I said you were like a dog. You know, a big dog might tear me into atoms.

GREENY. That is true, Master Fred. And it would not be very far from the truth if you had called me a dog. I am no better ; but I am not a biting, snarling dog. I never hurt anybody but myself. I suffer a good deal, boys ; dogs do n't suffer. (*Here he covers his face.*)

FRED. Will you tell us something of your boyhood, Mr. Greeny ?

GREENY. Yes ; I was a puppy then. And it all lies in this ; you can want to know no more.

FRED. We do, Mr. Greeny ; tell us all about it.

GREENY. (*Takes a soiled daguerreotype and letter from his pocket and gives them to* FRED.) Read — read. 'T is my mother's letter. I was her loved child once — I am Poor Greeny now — worse than a dog, for a dog cannot remember.

FRED. (*Reads the letter.*) " My darling boy, dearer to me than life, my hand is too feeble to write; be good, be true, and we shall meet in heaven."

GREENY. (*Sobbing.*) Never—never! I have lost my mother; I have lost myself.

[*The boys look at the picture.*]

GEORGE. (*Aside.*) Can it be that Greeny was ever this beautiful boy?

GREENY. Yes, he was. Give me the picture and the letter; 't is all I have—I am lost. Poor Greeny; you said he was a tomfool for everbody; that is true enough. But he was n't born so, as this face shows. (*Holds up the picture.*) He made himself so. When his father sent him to school he played truant; he did n't like to study; he did n't like to work; he was an idle puppy and gnawed a bone; he is a dog now and the bone follows him. But he will be a faithful dog and do his errand. The boys are on the common, playing ball; they sent me here to say that you must hurry up, or you would not be there to hear your names called. What message shall I take back to them? You hear their whistle.

FRED. What would you advise us to do, Mr. Greeny?

GREENY. I can give you my experience of the thing. When I was of your age and heard a whistle like this, I was n't slow to follow it; my lessons stayed in the book, where they have since remained. Good evening, boys; I have shewed you what I was, you see what I am.

FRED. Stop, Mr. Greeny; do n't go yet. You have excited our curiosity without telling us your early history.

GREENY. You want to know of my boyhood; you want to know what has made me what I am. I was a good and happy *little* boy, with a clean frock and red shoes on. My mother died; I remember it; I remember her last kiss. After this, Aunt Deborah took care of me. She was proud of me. When company came, I stood up on the floor and spoke pieces and sung to them. When I was a larger boy, my father moved to the city, and I went to school. Here I met boys larger than I was, and they told such stories as poor old Greeny tells now. They did n't love their books; they played truant; and they whistled me to follow them. But their whistling could n't have harmed me had I not made a puppy of myself and followed them, and tasted all their bad dishes. Well, the time came when I got kicked, scolded and lashed by everybody I met. If you would not be what I am, do not follow a dog's whistle. My memory is gone, and I must go too. Good night, boys. (*He goes; in a moment, puts his head in at the door and whistles.*)

GEORGE. How ludicrous, after the sad tale he has given us! But, Fred, I must go, for I promised the boys I would be there this evening, and I suppose the keeping a promise helps to make a *boy.*

FRED. 'T is one of the first requisites.

GEORGE. To-morrow evening I will be here again, and we will talk of this subject more. Good night.

[*Exit.*

FRED. Poor Ned Greeny! I am glad he came in here to-night, for he illustrated my subject to George much better than I could. The lesson he has given us

will strengthen my purpose too.   I see six feet of bone
and muscle, with two large hands and two large feet
attached to it, do not make a man.   What does? is the
question to be solved.   Is it knowledge?   If it were
Lawyer Bates would be a man; but everybody calls
him a sot.   It must be knowledge brought into practice.   This definition will not do — for one may have a
knowledge of what is false.   Then I will say, 't is to
know the truth and obey it.   [*Exit.*

MORNING AND NIGHT.

Characters:

MRS. LOUISA HEART.   LUCY EATON.
SIDNEY, *her little Son.*   MISS BETSEY SHADE.
MARY BRIGHT.

MISS SHADE, sitting at a table, dressed in black. She wears a long black crape veil; leans her head on her hand. MARY BRIGHT, a little girl, sitting on a cricket, stringing beads.

[*Enter* LUCY EATON.]

LUCY. Miss Shade, mother wants you should come round and spend the evening with us. She is expecting a few cheerful friends in, and she thinks you would enjoy their society.

MISS SHADE. (*Tries to subdue her grief; wipes away her tears.*) Tell your mother I appreciate her kindness, but she must excuse me; I cannot visit this evening.

LUCY. O, Miss Shade, do come round. Miss Howard is to be there, and you know she is so social and cheerful too, one can never feel sad in her presence.

MISS S. That is one reason why I could n't come. To-morrow is the anniversary of my dear sister's death. Of course, the day will be sanctified to her memory. This evening I wish to devote exclusively to solemn meditations. Have you ever been into her chamber since she died?

LUCY. No; I was there the day before. I remember it is a pleasant room, looking upon the east. I would like to die in such a room.

MISS S. Miss Lucy, what an expression! But if you will call on me to-morrow I will shew you into the room; 't is just as when she died—the same candle stands there, half burnt in the candlestick; the withered flowers are on the table; withered rose leaves lie scattered on her pillow; there is nothing changed there. From her window you can see the marble monument. (*Here she covers her face; sobs aloud. Little Mary rests from her work.*)

MARY. Where is your sister, Miss Shade?

MISS S. (*Sobs more violently, then groans out.*) Blessed be the innocence of ignorance. *Where is she?* The breaking heart asks *where?* The minister preaches patience. He says, "time will bring relief." Such consolation is but mockery; as if it were a comfort to feel that Time, with his frosty touch, could deaden the affections. One whole year, Lucy, this aching heart of mine has asked the same question that little Mary asks this morning—*Where is she?* and mocking echo answers, *where?*

LUCY. I thought, Miss Shade, you were a Christian. Are you not a member of the church?

MISS S. Yes; I have been a member of it twelve years. I have been a Sunday school teacher. I have comforted many a mourner. But when sorrow enters our own dwelling, I find myself enveloped in darkness; my religion does not sustain me.

MARY. Where is your religion, Miss Shade?

MISS S. O, the child! Hush, Mary. My heart is sore; your enquiries make it writhe in agony. Where is my religion? Where? Mocking echo answers, *Where?* I might as well have been born and educated in a heathen land. I am enveloped in a shroud of night.

MARY. Have you no bible, Miss Shade?

MISS S. Yes, to be sure I have a bible, but it don't comfort me.

LUCY. Perhaps you don't believe what is written there.

MISS S. Yes, I do; indeed I do. I am not an infidel, by any means.

LUCY. Then why do you mourn for your sister as if she were dead? You know the bible is full of the doctrine of *life*. There is no death, only what sin brings: the simple throwing off these material bodies isn't death. We are in an embryo state here — never fully born until we are freed from this house of clay.

MISS S. Lucy, 't is one thing to talk, another to feel. You have never tasted sorrow.

[*Enter* MRS. HEART, *dressed in white, and little* SIDNEY *with a basket of flowers.*]

MRS. HEART. Lucy, I am glad to meet you. I want some of your assistance this morning. Bring your basket here, Sidney. We gathered these flowers from Mr. Day's garden. I think there are not white ones enough for the wreath. I should like to have you assist me in making it; my fingers are a little unsteady. I didn't sleep last night.

LUCY. What is the wreath for, Mrs. Heart?

MRS. H.   I thought you had heard of the angel visitor I had last night.

LUCY.   No, I 've heard nothing.   I 've just come into town.   I stayed with auntie yesterday.

MRS. H.   Last evening, when I laid my darling Lulu into the cradle, Sidney came in from the garden with a rosebud in his hand.   He brought it to me, whispering, "Is Lulu asleep?"   I said, "No."   Then he said, "Baby—Lulu!"   She opened her eyes, and smiled as only babies can smile.   Sidney put the sweet rosebud into her hand.   She grasped it tightly, and soon convulsively.   I sent for a physician.   He seemed greatly moved when he saw her, then gently told me my babe was in her last sleep.

SIDNEY.   We can 't wake her now ; only the angels can wake her up.   You must come in and see her ; she looks so pretty in her little silk cradle.   She keeps hold of the flower I gave her.

MRS. H.   Now, Lucy, I want you should help me make the wreath.   I shall have to go to the conservatory for some white flowers.   These that I have will do for the table, and some of them may do for the foot of the casket.   The others I want all white.   She is so purely beautiful in her innocence that white only will be suitable for her.

LUCY.   Mrs. Heart, let me go for the flowers while you rest you here.

MRS. H.   I will let you, Lucy, as I am feeling weary. Many of the friends at the house offered to go for me, but I chose to go myself.   It seemed as if my own hands must do this last office of love for the pretty casket that once held our baby. But I will rest here until you return, then we will arrange the wreath.

SIDNEY. Mother, I'm not tired; shall I go with Lucy to gather flowers for Lulu?

MRS. H. Yes, darling, you may go. Perhaps little Mary Bright would like to go too; she was one of Lulu's friends; Lulu loved her very much. Mary, would n't you like to go home with us, after we get the flowers, and see the pretty casket?

MARY. (*Puts away her beads.*) I should like it very much, and to go for the flowers too. My white rosebush has six buds on it and two roses. May I give them to Lulu?

SIDNEY. O yes, Mary, you may; we may give her anything now. The angels have put her to sleep, and they will wake her in the morning; then she will be with them in heaven.

MARY. Won't she come back here any more?

SIDNEY. No, she 'll never wake up here again.

MARY. And shall we never see her again?

SIDNEY. O yes, we shall see her when the angels put us to sleep. They put us to sleep when we get sick. Last night my head ached, and I laid still; I thought the angels were there and were going to put me to sleep, just as they did Lulu?

MARY. Were you frightened, Sidney?

SIDNEY. No; angels could n't frighten me; you know they are always good. But when I thought they were going to take me, I felt the tears coming. I wanted they should take me, but I wanted they should take mamma too.

MARY. And did n't you want they should take your papa?

SIDNEY. I did n't think about papa then. Yes, I should want him to be with us. Papa do n't like it because they have taken Lulu; he stays in his room.

MARY. I should n't like it either. When I come to your house, I shall want to see the baby. 'T will be lonesome there now.

SIDNEY. Yes, 't will be lonesome. I 'm going to borrow Mrs. Dike's baby sometimes; 't is n't so pretty as Lulu; there 's no baby so pretty as our darling Lulu was.

MARY. And I think it was too bad for the angels to take her.

SIDNEY. No, Mary, 't was n't too bad; you know they brought her to us — she was a little tiny baby then. She had no teeth. How she did grow! and how much she did learn! She could say, Idney; and she could take hold of my frock and walk about the room. O little Lulu! sometime I shall go to see her, and mamma will go too.

MRS. H. If Lucy is ready, and Mary has got her beads put away, you had better go for the flowers. We shall have none too much time to arrange them. Mary must go home with Sidney, and he can tell her many things about our darling Lulu.

LUCY. I am ready. Mrs. Heart, I would like to introduce you to Miss Shade.

[MISS SHADE *raises her veil, slowly rises, and solemnly shakes hands.*]

MRS. H. I am happy to see you, Miss Shade. My heart goes forth with a bound this morning to meet everybody.

Miss S. Perhaps it will recoil on approaching me, for I am wrapped in the gloom of midnight darkness. I see no light, I feel no joy.

Mrs. H. No, it doth not recoil. Its pulsation is quickened with the desire to lead you from the darkness of night to the brightness of a new morning. Why will you sit thus, nourishing a morbid and selfish grief?

Miss S. (*Groans.*) You speak severely.

Mrs. H. I speak truly and earnestly. I say, life is too precious to be spent in selfish mourning. Only a few more seasons shall have their round, and our work on earth is finished — our book of life is complete, the lids are sealed. All useless then will be our regrets to find so many pages a blank, or, what may be worse, stained with selfish tears.

Miss S. Mrs. Heart, you speak as one that hath never tasted sorrow. And yet I am aware that the king of terrors, with his frowning visage, was at your door this morning, and robbed your home of its dearest treasure.

Mrs. H. You are mistaken. You are enveloped in the shadows of night, and see nothing clearly. There hath been no king of terrors at our door; there has been no robbing of our home's dearest treasure. One year ago our Heavenly Father gave us a beautiful babe, and He gave us a heaven of love with it. This morning, with the rising of the sun, He sent one of His purest angels to translate the precious little one to a higher state of existence.

Miss S. And does it not seem like a cruel mockery to bestow a precious gift, and then recall it so soon?

Mrs. H. It would seem so were this the all of life. But since we have learned that this is but the embryo of existence, we know our loved ones are not taken from us when they lay aside their material garments. My darling babe! I miss her from my arms, but she was never so warmly cradled in my heart as now. The love I feel for her is intense; and I know her baby spirit will draw me more and more to a spiritual life. I have already learned a lesson that leads onward and upward. I have learned a lesson of trust.

Miss S. How differently doth grief affect us! I have learned despair.

Mrs. H. The lesson we learn is of our own choosing. The Lord hath brought to your mind and mine the great doctrine of life. His revelations are wonderful — beyond what finite minds can fully grasp. Yet we see enough. We know our Heavenly Father's inmost life is love; and the form of this love is wisdom; and thus, in His dealings with His children, He cannot err. It remains with us whether we trust Him or whether we rebel.

Miss S. I wish I had your faith, Mrs. Heart.

Mrs. H. That is impossible. My faith is not transferable; and were it so, it would not be adapted to you. The Lord hath given you an understanding of your own. Do not close your eyes; do not seal your heart against His coming. Listen to His words: "Come unto me, all ye that labor and are heavy laden, and I will give you rest."

Miss S. I would be glad to go unto Him, but the way is closed up. All about me is night.

Mrs. H. All about me is morning — bright, beautiful morning. I feel as if I were with my darling child, and born into a new life. Natural desires, fears and questionings are hushed. The " I Am " is the All; in Him I trust. Wonderful is His power, and as wonderful His love. One year ago, all unasked, He gave me heaven in my babe. He is the same infinite love now as then, and I will trust Him. " He is my Refuge and Fortress."

Miss S. You will not always feel it bright morning, Mrs. Heart. This present excitement will pass away, and long hours of desolation will come.

Mrs. H. Your words may prove true, and they must if I let go my hold of the great Fountain of Life. If I rely upon self, if I view things from a natural vision only, desolation is mine.

Miss S. And that is the condition I am in, Mrs. Heart. All is night.

Mrs. H. The Bible says, " He that abideth in the secret place of the Most High shall not be afraid of the terror by night." I think you have wandered off into a far country, and are feeding on husks that swine do eat, Miss Shade.

Miss S. It is so, and I am dying with hunger : tell me how to return.

Mrs. H. Be a child again. Jesus takes little children in His arms and blesses them. Suffer yourself to go unto Him. You remember when the Lord called little Samuel, he answered, " Here am I, for Thou didst call me."

Miss S. And if I heard His voice, I believe I would make the same answer.

Mrs. H. In removing from your natural vision your

loved sister, He calls you to come up higher. Listen to His voice, and seek not the living among the dead.

Miss S.   How shall I take the first step?

Mrs. H.   "If ye know these things, happy are ye if ye *do* them."

Miss S.   Night still—tell me how to do them.

Mrs. H.   Jesus says, " Take up your bed and walk."

Miss S.   More and more dark.

Mrs. H.   Live the heavenly doctrines. Crucify within you every selfish feeling. Come forth into active life. Be a child—obedient, humble and trustful. Put yourself into the loving stream of Providence; take the oars in your hand, and earnestly work, not only your own way, but help all others that you find grounded in the miry clay of earth.

[*Enter Lucy and the children, with flowers.*]

Sidney.   Mamma, all these for dear Lulu. Let us go home now and carry them to her.

Mrs. H.   Yes, we will go home. Can you go with us, Lucy?

Lucy.   I am much pleased to go. Let me remain with you a few days. I shall rest and grow strong in your home.

Mrs. H.   Miss Shade, will you walk round and see my baby's casket? You will not see *her*, but you may feel an influence there that may help you on to childhood again.

Miss S.   Thank you. The night has become tedious; I shall be glad to break from it.

Mrs. H.   Blessed are they that do His commandments, that they may have right to the tree of life, and may enter in through the gates into the city. [*Exeunt.*

THE BOOTBLACK.

Characters:

TOM DICKENS.   MR. DAYBRIGHT.

HEZEKIAH EARNEST.   SUSIE DAYBRIGHT, *his Niece.*

NICHOLAS FLASH.

TOM (*alone*). Am I a bootblack? (*Places his hand upon his head, and walks across the stage absorbed in thought.*) Am I a bootblack? Two years ago, I walked the streets, with brush in hand, crying at the top of my voice, " Boots to black ! Boots to black ! " and when some dusty traveler would pause in his way, and permit me to shine his boots, then give me a few pennies, more or less, according to the warmth of his heart, I was gratefully contented, and in sincerity said, " Thank ye, sir." But, *to-day*, when Nick Flash stuck up his boot, and tauntingly said, " Here is a job for you, my boy; put on the shine." I felt like knocking him down — my honor was insulted ; but I only called him a contemptuous snob, and passed on.

[*Enter* NICHOLAS FLASH.]

NICK. Yes, you did call me a snob, and you shall answer for it. Meet me this evening, in Mr. Daybright's back yard, and I will teach you manners.

TOM. It would be more agreeable to me to meet

you in Mr. Daybright's parlor. I am engaged to pass the evening there, and have a game of chess with Susie?

NICK. *You,* son of a drunkard! *You,* dirty boot-black! Play chess with Susie Daybright! The stars have fallen from heaven — let the darkness of night cover us.

TOM. It does not take very clear vision to observe that the darkness of night hath covered Nick. Flash. I might have been mistaken in calling him a snob, for, really, he has made himself so obscure that one cannot tell what he is. I will withdraw my proposal to meet you in Mr. Daybright's parlor. It would be quite out of place, as he only receives gentlemen there.

NICK. Meet me in the park, and I will put you where you will never insult a gentleman's son again.

TOM. There is some difference between a gentleman's son and the son of a gentleman.

NICK. I see none.

TOM. The world, society, respects a gentleman's son; but when the world, society, meets the son of a gentleman, and finds him ill-bred, presuming, overbearing, they set a mark on him.

NICK. You impudent bootblack! I'll black your face.

TOM. The mark is on you. One loses sight of the advantage you might possess by being rocked in a gentleman's cradle. You call me a boot-black, the son of a drunkard. I was a bootblack — I was the son of a drunkard; but one may rise as well as fall. I helped to black boots in the early part of my life; I am strong now, and resolute to climb the hill, although the path is steep, and strewn with thorns that sometimes make my feet bleed.

NICK. You, Tom Dickens, rise! You, the bootblack, the son of a drunkard, talk of rising! Your gas may inflate you for a day, but the bursting will come, then down you go into a ditch lower than the one you started from.

TOM. Yes; I, Tom Dickens, talk of rising.

NICK. I suppose you are looking up to the highest pinnacle of fame.

TOM. I am looking up to something more substantial than fame. Fame often proves itself a bubble. I would not waste the energies of youth seeking it. But I am looking *up*—I have set my mark high. As I said, I am climbing a steep, thorny hill; and if, on my way, I meet Nick Flash coming down, I will step one side and let him pass. I do not choose to meet him in any park, to give him an opportunity of blacking my face. That is lower business than blacking boots. How many pennies would you charge for the job?

NICK. (*Takes a pistol from his pocket.*) Idiot, do you know what this is? Do you know its name? Do you know its power?

'TOM. Yes, I know its name and its power; and I know gentlemen's sons sometimes fall so low from their honorable birthright as to purchase the use of the hangman's rope with such a toy as you hold in your hand.

(NICK *holds the pistol up. Enter* SUSIE DAYBRIGHT.)

SUSIE. Nicholas Flash! what have you in your hand?

NICK.   A pistol.   Any harm in it?

SUSIE.   You were pointing it at the head of my friend.

NICK.   *Your friend!*

SUSIE.   What does it mean?

NICK.   It means, that dirty, cowardly bootblack has insulted me.   It means, the dastardly son of a drunkard has insulted the son of a gentleman.

SUSIE.   Give me that pistol, or I will report you to the sheriff.   You know the law punishes every one that carries a loaded pistol in his pocket.   Nicholas Flash, give me the pistol!

NICK.   I am afraid to trust you with it, your eyes flash fire.

SUSIE.   *Give it to me!*   Then, I will tell you my errand.   (NICK *reaches it towards her.*)   I am afraid to touch the wicked thing.   Tom, please take it for me, and throw it out of the window.

NICK.   You don't suppose that cowardly idiot would dare touch this pistol, do you?

SUSIE.   Don't call names, Nick; the habit is disgraceful; but let Tom take the pistol.

NICK.   That means, let him take my life.

TOM.   You are mistaken.   I would not harm you. I would step one side to let you pass.

SUSIE.   Nick, what are you going to do with that awful pistol?

NICK.   Put it in my pocket.   You need n't be afraid of it, since it is not loaded.   I only carry it to frighten drunkards' sons, and keep bootblacks in their place.

SUSIE.   O, Nick, I am ashamed to own you as a

cousin. What makes you disgrace yourself so? Your poor mother! How it would grieve her, if she knew you were attempting to pull down an orphan boy that is trying to rise! Shame on you!

NICK. He is rising too fast. Uncle Daybright is doing too much for him.

SUSIE. Not a bit. Tom is working hard himself, and we will help him all we can.

NICK. You say *we* — *we* will help him. Who do you mean by *we?*

SUSIE. Only uncle and I. I will do everything I can for Tom, while he is doing so much for himself. I do n't care if he has been a bootblack. He shines all the brighter for it now. 'T is true, his father was a drunkard; but it is shameful in you, Nick Flash, to speak of this to him. It is not his fault. The memory of it is painful enough, and the reality was more so. Shame on you, Nicholas Flash!

NICK. I am sorry to feel your displeasure, Susie.

SUSIE. I would not be worthy the name I bear, were I not displeased with you now, Nick; and I am going to punish you. I came round here to invite you to visit us this evening; we are going to have a few friends in; but I withhold the invitation.

NICK. Are you going to invite the bootblack?

SUSIE. I am not going to invite the blockhead, Flash; and I will not answer his question, unless he puts it in gentlemanly language.

NICK. As you say, Susie. Now, are you going to invite *Mr. Dickens* to your party to-night?

SUSIE. He is already invited.

NICK. Then, your withholding an invitation from me, is of no account, for I should not disgrace myself by attending a party where a bootblack was present.

SUSIE. Nick, apologize to Tom, or I will cut you in the street.

NICK. The apology will come better after his explosion.

SUSIE. Nicholas Flash, your mother wants you. Go, confess your wickedness to her.

NICK. Gentle Susie, I obey. Good night. Thanks for your kindness.   [*Exit.*

SUSIE. Tom, what does all this mean? What has happened? Why is Nick making a fool of himself?

TOM. I cannot answer that question. One hour ago, as I was coming across the bridge, I stopped to look at your uncle's noble vessel, as it came near the shore. There was a fine breeze; the sails were all filled, and it moved so gracefully through the parting water, I could not help giving it a welcome cheer. Nick was standing by. I had not noticed him, as there were many others crowded together on the bridge. As I cheered, Nick stuck his dirty boot up into my face, and sneeringly said, "Tom, shine my boot." I felt the insult. The crowd hissed and laughed, whether at him or me, I don't know. I was angry, and could have thrown him into the water; I am strong enough to do it, but I only called him a contemptuous snob, and walked away. He followed me — you know the rest. But, Miss Daybright, do not give it a thought. I would sooner be thrown into the water myself, than cause one shadow to cross your path.

Susie. I am ashamed of Nicholas; but do n't mind him, Tom. Your way is opening bright. Little Lucy Grey was in at uncle's this morning. Do you know her?

Tom. I have seen her.

Susie. How many times?

Tom. Only twice.

Susie. Do you know her mother?

Tom. I have seen her once. They are poor people. I feel sorry for them.

Susie. We know you do. What did you do with that gold dollar uncle gave you at Christmas?

Tom. Was it not mine, to do what I chose with?

Susie. To be sure it was. Why have you got your hand wrapped up in a handkerchief?

Tom. A dog bit it, but not badly.

Susie. Tom, I know the whole story, and I would sooner have a bootblack for my brother, than the veriest prince that ever lived. Was n't you afraid the dog was mad?

Tom. I never thought of such a thing.

Susie. You are a brave boy; a coward would have thought of it. Were you frightened when Nick drew his pistol? (The wicked boy!)

Tom. No; I have suffered too much in my life to be afraid of an unloaded pistol.

Susie. But you did not know it was unloaded, and you did not know the dog was n't mad.

Tom. Susie, we get along better in life not to think of danger. Do what we see to do, and that is all there is of it.

SUSIE. So you fought that savage dog, and saved little Lucy's life. Uncle is going to have a doctor examine the wound, to see if there is poison in it. Why did you give her the gold dollar?

TOM. They are very poor. She had no shoes. Lucy is a nice girl. But the dog is n't mad; he is only a cross old cur. His master calls him so.

SUSIE. Tom, Uncle Daybright is away from home most of the time. Auntie and I have no one to drive us out when we want to ride.

TOM. I think your Cousin Nicholas would hold the lines safely for you.

SUSIE. Nick has disgraced himself; and that is n't all, uncle wants a boy to stay with us all the time, and I want a brother. I want some one that is n't afraid of mad dogs nor pistols.

TOM. You would not want a bootblack?

SUSIE. You are not a bootblack.

TOM. Only two years ago, I walked the streets crying, "Boots to black! Boots to black!" And I might be in the same black business now, but for the kindness of you and your uncle.

SUSIE. But you are not a bootblack now, Tom. That belongs to the past.

TOM. It seems to me there is no past; all is in the now. I am continually haunted with the question, *Am I a bootblack?* You know we learn from books that nothing, either in the natural or spiritual world, is ever destroyed, only changes come. That flower in your hand was once a bud — the bud is not destroyed now, only changed, or grown to a flower.

SUSIE. Well, Tom, I want a brother that thinks. You and I were once babies — where are the babies now?

TOM. Changed, or grown, or developed, as you may please to call it. The baby is still in us, and we must take good care of it. All the innocence, all the good, all the love we have, belong to the baby in us.

SUSIE. Tom, when did you ever find time to think so much?

TOM. When I was a bootblack, waiting in the streets for something to do, until my very bones ached. 'T was when I was a bootblack, too, that I learned to pity those that were worse off than myself. In that hard, miserable life, I learned many other lessons — they are a part of myself. So, now say, Miss Daybright, am I not still a bootblack?

SUSIE. Do not call me Miss Daybright. Call me Susie, that is more like a brother.

TOM. Thank you for the privilege. Then, Susie, am I not a bootblack still?

SUSIE. I will not answer that question until I have thought it over ten thousand times. 'T is a big question. I do not like to think as well as you do. I give it up — be it as you say. If you are a bootblack, then I want a bootblack for a brother. But here is uncle coming.

[*Enter* MR. DAYBRIGHT.]

MR. DAYBRIGHT. Thomas, I was looking for you. I want some one to come into my family and make his home there. Will you fill the vacancy?

TOM. I would like to, if I can be of use to you.

MR. DAYBRIGHT. That you can. I have seen Mr.

Orr, and he is willing to take some one else to fill your place in his store. Come round with Susie to supper, and we'll arrange everything satisfactorily.

[*Exit* MR. DAYBRIGHT.

SUSIE. Now, Tom, I told you your way was brightening — and I have a brother. I will let you do all the thinking.

TOM. And what will you do?

SUSIE. I will draw conclusions.

TOM. I am afraid there is some truth in what Nicholas said, "Your uncle is doing too much for me."

SUSIE. Not a bit. I will begin now to draw conclusions from your thinking. You said, a few moments ago, that we get along better in life not to think of danger — do what we see to do, and there is the all of it. Now, you have only to come to uncle's, and be his child and my brother, and that is the all of it.

[*Enter* HEZEKIAH EARNEST.]

HEZEKIAH. Tom Dickens, I have a message for you.

TOM. I am ready for it.

HEZEKIAH. Nicholas Flash wants you to meet him in the park to-night, at seven o'clock. Will you be there?

TOM. Give my compliments to Mr. Flash, and tell him I will step aside and let him pass me. I have not time to meet him in the park this evening.

HEZEKIAH. But he is in earnest.

TOM. So am I.

SUSIE. Go and tell Nick, his Cousin Susie will meet him there at six o'clock. Tell him she will have the choice of weapons — to leave his wicked pistol at home. Hezekiah, will you tell him this?

HEZEKIAH. If you command it. Allow me to ask what weapon you intend to bring? since I am his second.

SUSIE. I will bring a weapon that will shame my insolent cousin into an ash heap.

HEZEKIAH. I will beg to be excused from being his second, then. [*Exit* HEZEKIAH.

SUSIE. Cousin Nick! I am ashamed of him, and I will make him ashamed of himself. Come, Tom, we shall find our supper ready, let's go home. You are a brave boy; and if you claim to be the blossom of a bootblack, 't is all the same, I claim you for a brother. (SUSIE *takes his arm.*)

[*Curtain falls.*]

BLIND EVA.

Characters:

EVA; SADIE, *her Sister;* LOTTIE; BESSIE; *and* TOM, BESSIE's *Brother.*

Curtain rises. Blind EVA, dressed in white, is kneeling, with hands clasped, as if in prayer. A moment of silence, then she devoutly speaks.

EVA. How rich is life! How full of blessings! O, our Heavenly Father is not only *great*, but so good! The bible says, " He covereth Himself with light as a garment; He stretcheth out the heavens like a curtain; He layeth the beams of His chambers in the waters; He maketh the clouds His chariot; He walketh upon the wings of the wind." All this is true. This is His *greatness*. It seems far, far off, beyond our reach. But the bible says again, He is love; He watches over the fall of sparrows; He takes little children in His arms and blesses them. And this is not far off; 't is just here, 't is all about us; 't is within us. I feel it here. (*Lays her hand on her heart.*) This love makes Him our Father; we can rest safely in His arms.

[*Enter* SADIE. *She tenderly places her hand on* EVA's *cheek.*]

SADIE. How came you here alone, Sister Eva?

EVA. I am not alone, dear Sadie; a company of bright angels were with me when you came in. But I am glad you have come. (*Taking her hand.*) I so love to feel this precious hand. How soft and warm it is! Is it not the most perfect of all God's works?

SADIE. (*Caressing* EVA, *leads her to a chair and sits down on a cricket near her.*) I do not see anything wonderful in my hand, it is good to work with; it can dust the room, knit a little, sew a little, and tend baby.

EVA. O, it does much more than that. It is my eyes in this dark world. (*Kisses it.*) 'T is through this precious hand that half my blessings come. How happy I feel when it rests on my cheek. 'T is my light, my music, my poetry; my very heart dances when I feel it—there is a wonderful concentration of life in the hand.

[*Enter* BESSIE *and* LOTTIE.]

BESSIE. O, Lottie, I am glad to be here with you. I am tired of brother Tom. He just worries the life out of me. How rough boys are! Sometimes I wish I had no brother.

LOTTIE. Don't say so Bessie; I'd give my head if I had a brother like Tom. I like him.

BESSIE. Give your heart, and you may have him altogether. He just torments the life out of me. O, he's a great hector.

[*Enter* TOM.]

TOM. (*Pulls* BESSIE's *hair.*) Miss Midget Fussy, will you give a kind word to your brother to-day?

BESSIE. No, Tom; and I wish you would go away from here; I want to have a good time with Lottie.

TOM. So do I. I wish Lottie was my sister; she would n't play Miss Fussy as you do.

BESSIE. She would play somebody else, if you should strike her as you did me this morning.

TOM. Hush, Bessie! Do n't tell that story; 't was only a sweet love pat I gave you.

BESSIE. *A love pat!* Much like it. My ear burns now with the blow you gave me.

TOM. Miss Midget Fussy, I love you too well to strike you with this big hand of mine, unless you make me tiger-angry by cutting my kite string to fasten some of your trappings with. My kite is my pet; and when you cut the string, look out for the consequence.

BESSIE. You are a rough boy, Tom, and forever in the way. You did n't brush your hair this morning; how like a fright you look.

TOM. Do I look bad, Lottie? You see, sister Midget is forever pecking me. Won't she go for " woman's rights " when she gets her trail on? She is practising on me. Now say something kind to me, Lottie. Do I look awful bad?

LOTTIE. Did you ever see a porcupine, Tom?

TOM. Now, Lottie (*smoothing down his hair*), I thought you were my friend.

LOTTIE. So I am; and just before you came in, I said I wished you were my brother. But, Tom, if you were, I would n't let you strike me.

TOM. Strike *you!* Who would ever think of striking *you,* Lottie? I would much sooner kiss you.

LOTTIE. Well, were I your sister, you might. But I should brush your hair first. I would n't have a porcupine kissing me, if he were my brother.

BESSIE. O, Lottie, you are my friend. Give rough Tom what he deserves.

LOTTIE. I always give everyone what they deserve. I like Tom ; but he shall brush his hair, and he sha'n't strike you. Now go, Tom, and wash your hand clean from its sinfulness, and smooth down your porcupine feathers.

TOM. There is a bit of the donkey in me — I can't be driven.

EVA. Thomas will you not speak to your blind friend ?

TOM. (*Giving* EVA *his hand.*) Yes, Eva ; and I should have spoken to you before, had not these two girls began pecking me.

EVA. (*Holding his hand between hers.*) Tom, your hand is a good one ; I like to hold it ; but 't is not so soft and gentle as Sadie's.

TOM. Well, Eva, you should n't expect that, since I am a boy.

EVA. But boys have good warm hands, Tom. They may not be as soft and gentle as girls', but they may be just as warm and good. And yours is a good one. I like to feel it. How wonderfully it is made ! All the fingers there, and the thumb, too ! And the joints — not one of them is missing. How many good things this hand can do, with its fingers so nicely jointed.

TOM. It can do some bad things, too.

EVA. I should n't think it could ; it feels very warm.

TOM. You make it warm, Eva. Bessie calls it cold and hard.

EVA.   I do not make it warm, Tom; 't is your warm heart that gives it the glow.

TOM.   Do you think I have a warm heart, Eva?

EVA.   Certainly I do.   I know you have.   I feel its warmth every time you come near me.

TOM.   These girls here do n't think I have a warm heart, or a good one.   Lottie calls me a porcupine.

LOTTIE.   I think, Tom, you have a good heart, and a warm one too.   You do n't comb your hair but once a year, so I said you looked like something with ruffled feathers.

BESSIE.   And I never said, brother Tom, and I never thought it either, that you had n't a good heart; but you are rough, and your good heart finds fun in teasing your sister.   You call me Midget and Fussy.

TOM.   I can 't well help speaking the truth.   I never call Eva such names, and she sees no resemblance in me to a porcupine; do you, Eva?

EVA.   Indeed, Tom, I do n't.   People call me blind —you call me blind—yet I have a sight more correct than yours, Bessie's, or Lottie's; and that sight tells me, and it tells truly, that not one of the porcupine's sharp quills belongs to your nature.

BESSIE.   But his bushy head looks like one; Lottie says so.

EVA.   I think people are unfortunate in having eyes to see the outer form of a thing.   It sometime deceives them, and often leads the mind from true internal thinking.   Now, here is your brother Tom, we are all agreed that he has a good warm heart; but you and Lottie, with your eyes, see him looking like a porcupine, and his rough ways annoy you. Without eyes, I see Tom a noble boy; he is the perfect embodiment of a good and true heart. I like to have him near me; I like to hear him talk; I like to take his hand — he has a good one.

BESSIE. But he struck me with it this morning, Eva.

EVA. (*Looking sad.*) O, Bessie, are you not mistaken? Have not your eyes deceived you?

BESSIE. If my eyes deceived me, my sense of feeling did n't.

EVA. I do not think this hand could strike; it feels so warm and kind. Somebody or something must have compelled it to do that which is entirely foreign to its nature.

TOM. I suppose, Eva, I compelled it.

EVA. I do n't think you did, Tom; your heart is too kind to compel this hand to do such a wicked thing. Try, see if you can strike me. (*Lets go his hand.*)

TOM. I could die easier.

EVA. Try and see if you can strike Bessie or Lottie.

TOM. Not now, I can 't; but if they make me angry enough, I could.

EVA. Then is it you or them that makes the hand strike?

TOM. You will have to answer your own wise question, little preacher.

EVA. Well, 't is not very easy to answer. By this I mean, it is not very easy to make you understand it. You look upon the outer world, I look upon the inner; you see the effect, I see the cause. In the inner world I see many bright lights; I see all kinds of feelings

there, too. Perhaps you will understand me better if
I compare these feelings to animals, for in spirit they
are like them. I see there the lion, tiger and fox; I see
also the calf, lamb and dove. Sometimes these animals
all lie still, and sometimes the fierce animals try to destroy the gentle and innocent ones. Sometimes they
all seem to be asleep, then we feel dull and stupid;
again, some one of them wakes up, and we are all alive.
I see now, in Tom, the innocent lamb, awake and sport-
ing on a green lawn; the dove is cooing her sweet song,
and this makes his voice sound melodious when he
speaks.

Toм. What animal did Bessie wake up in me that
made this hand strike her?

Eva. I think it was the tiger. Had I been present
and heard your voice at the time the savage deed was
done, I could tell for a certainty—the sound of the
voice never deceives.

Toм. Bessie ought to be cautious, not to wake up
such ferocious animals.

Eva. Yes, Bessie ought to be cautious about this;
but sometimes they wake very easily, and sometimes
they get tired of sleeping, and wake of themselves, and
begin prowling round to see what mischief they can do.

Toм. And what can we do in that case?

Eva. Always keep them chained. Never let them
breathe one breath in the outer world of active life.
The moment you feel one of them stir, crush it, suffo-
cate it. This is easily done when the first motion is
felt; but let any one of these wild beasts get a little
start, and the madhouse will scarcely hold them.

Tom. Do you ever feel any of these ferocious animals troubling your peaceful life, Eva?

Eva. Yes, Tom, they are there, but I do not give them the liberty you do yours. What you call my blindness has turned my thoughts much into the inner world, and I always keep a strong guard there. Sadie's hand helps me in my work, too.

Sadie. And I came for you, Eva, to go into the parlor; ma wants to see you.

Eva. (*Takes* Sadie's *hand.*) Good evening. Take care of the wild beasts, Tom; keep them chained.

[*Exeunt.*

Tom. What an angel blind Eva is! And how wise and good! She sees things truly; she sees rough Tom as he is, in her presence the wild beasts all asleep. Bessie rouses the tiger, and Lottie sees the porcupine quills. Good night, girls. [*Exit.*

Lottie. Well, Bessie, we must go; 't is getting late; to-morrow we will go round and see Eva. I should like to hear her tell what she sees in me. I think the dog is there. [*Exeunt.*

THE MAY-BASKET ARMY.

Characters:

LUCY WHITE,   JANE BLUE,   JOHN DIX,
MARY PINK,   DOLLY BLACK,   JOSEPH RAY,
                              THOMAS DIKE.

Four little girls, dressed in White, Pink, Blue, and Black, seated at a table strewn with tissue paper. Each little girl has a May-basket.

[*Enter their* TEACHER. *The children rise and approach her with their baskets.*]

TEACHER. My dear girls, I am delighted to see you altogether here. 'T is pleasanter and more social making your baskets in company. Are they complete?

PINK. We had just finished them as you came in; and we have been so happy in making them. Are they not pretty?

TEACHER. They are very beautiful. Please hold them all up so that I can see them. The pattern is the same, but the colors different.

PINK. Yes; I made mine pink, or perhaps it is red, because that is my favorite color. You know the sun is always red when it is warm; and blushes are red, and blushes come straight from the heart, and love is in the heart, so I think love is red, and love is the best thing in the world: the Bible says so.

TEACHER. Where did you find that in the Bible?

PINK. Well, the Bible says, "God is love."

TEACHER. Yes, my dear child, "God is love," and

204

love is the best thing in the world; and 't is love makes heaven.

PINK. I know that. Grandma and our baby are all love; and Auntie says they are our heaven.

BLUE. I made mine blue, teacher, because the sky is blue, and blue is the most beautiful color there is.

TEACHER. And why do you think blue the most beautiful color?

BLUE. I cannot tell. But I never tire looking at the beautiful sky. I see the sun there, and all the stars, and the moon. And when those light, fleecy clouds go sailing by, I think bright angels are in them.

WHITE. I made mine white because you told me innocence and purity were clothed in white. Then white, you know, always looks so bright and clean. Little lambs are white, and little babies are dressed in white, and I love them. Everything white looks so pure.

TEACHER. You three have made a good selection of colors; but how is it with Blackey? She looks like a dark shadow here.

BLACK. O, teacher, I made my basket black on purpose. You see 't is made of coarse paper, and just put together anyway. I am going to give it to Phœbe Doler. Phœbe is a coarse girl, and rough in her manners, and she has an ugly face, and they are poor people.

TEACHER. Is this a good reason for giving her a coarse, ugly May-basket?

BLACK. I should think so; it looks just like her.

TEACHER. (*Takes the basket and examines it.*) What an ugly basket this is! Who could have made a thing so entirely devoid of all beauty?

BLACK. I made it. But then I made it for Phœbe Doler.

TEACHER. Blackey, I do not understand you. You are not a bad girl; you have not a bad heart; and I do not understand how you could have made so bad a basket.

BLACK. O, I made it for Phœbe Doler.

TEACHER. It makes no difference who you made it for, since it is a gift; and a gift is a child of the heart. I did not think your heart could send forth into the world such an ugly child.

BLACK. But it is for Phœbe Doler.

TEACHER. Phœbe Doler did n't make this basket. It is your child; you made it; and I am pained that you should allow such a bad feeling in your heart to take form and come forth into the world. Do you think it as pretty as Pinkey's.

BLACK. Not half; but then, it is for Phœbe Doler.

TEACHER. Do you think Phœbe Doler is pretty?

BLACK. No, she has an ugly face; 't is covered with freckles.

TEACHER. And, you say, your basket looks just like her. I saw, this morning, an ugly weed growing in my garden. I pulled it up and burned it.

BLACK. And would you burn this basket?

TEACHER. I would, by all means; and then I would watch my heart very closely, and never again let it give form to anything that was not beautiful.

[*Exit* BLACK.

[*Enter three Boys, with bonnets and shawls on.*]

JOHN. Teacher, we heard of this May army, and

so we procured ourselves uniforms, and have come to ask your permission to enlist as soldiers.

TEACHER. The addition of so many "braves" to our army would increase our strength. Your uniform may answer; but there are other things necessary to fit you for a place in our ranks.

JOSEPH. We were aware of this, and have come prepared. Question us, if you please.

TEACHER. Do you know we are a May-basket army?

ALL. We do.

TEACHER. Are you prepared with baskets for an evening's march?

ALL. We are.

TEACHER. The spirit of our army is, to bless. Is there a blessing in your baskets?

ALL. We believe so.

TEACHER. I see no objections to your entering our ranks, but I will leave the decision to Pinkey.

PINK. We will not accept them until we see their baskets. [*Exeunt boys.*

BLUE. That was a wise decision, Pinkey: those boys looked full of mischief, with their bonnets on.

WHITE. But they are good boys. Sammy Ray would never do a wicked thing.

[*Re-enter boys.*]

JOHN. (*With a basketful of potatoes.*) Will not this basket of roots be a blessing to poor Mrs. Castaway?

TEACHER. Indeed it will. You have complied with the spirit of our army ; and though we see no delicate beauty in your rough basket, we know a living beauty is in the heart of it.

JOSEPH. My basket has a turkey in it. It is to go with the potatoes to Mrs. Castaway, for a bit of a relish.

TEACHER. A double blessing for the poor woman. You " braves " will give strength to our army. Your baskets are substantial. Now for Soldier Third.

THOMAS. My basket is a small one, and yet it contains what may be converted into tea, coffee, candles or snuff, as poor Mrs. Castaway may choose. (*He pours upon the table a hundred pennies.*)

TEACHER. The poor woman will not think she is a castaway when she finds this trio of gifts at her door. Now, Pinkey, what is your decision ? Shall we receive these bonneted volunteers into our army, or not ?

PINK. O, yes, we will receive them, but not their bonnets. I fear mischief in those comical bonnets.

BLUE. Do n't be over particular, Pinkey. You mistake a little innocent fun for mischief. Since their baskets are all right, do n't mind their bonnets.

THOMAS. There is no mischief in our bonnets. Are they not after the same pattern as your own ? Are they not in uniform ?

PINK. Uniform is not always harmony. Bonnets do not harmonize with your heavy baskets, neither do they harmonize with your boy-nature. Teacher, order them to take off their bonnets.

TEACHER. Pinkey, since you and Bluey differ in this matter of bonnets, we will let Whitey decide.

WHITE. I am so much pleased with this addition of substantiality to our army, that I would like to indulge these generous volunteers in all their sportive whims.

THOMAS. White fairy! your wish is our law. You have only to speak, and we obey.

WHITE. Thank you, good soldier. We girls do not like apes; but we like *boys*. (*The boys lay their bonnets at her feet.*)

PINK. Bravo, boys! that is well done. Now all is right. I'll pick up your bonnets, and keep them for some poor girls that have none.

[*Enter* BLACK, *smiling, dressed in scarlet, with a scarlet basket; all gently applaud.*]

TEACHER. The dark cloud has given place to a warm glowing sunbeam. Now you have a beautiful basket; the heart is all right; this one will please poor Phœbe Doler.

BLACK. I know it will. I don't think she ever had a pretty thing given to her in all her life. Perhaps it will do her good. I will try it, any way.

TEACHER. This trying it will do you good.

BLACK. And don't you think it will do Phœbe Doler good too?

TEACHER. Certainly I do. Every kind word spoken, and every beautiful or useful gift carries a blessing in its heart.

PINK. I am delighted with our May-basket army. Susie Blackey has changed to Scarlet. All is right; and I know how to manage the affair. We must hang our baskets on the door knob, then ring the bell and run. We must go in the evening, so that the darkness will conceal us.

BLUE. That's the way to do it, Pinkey — angels never shew themselves when they leave a gift.

THOMAS.   When shall we commence our march?

PINK.   As soon as you have gathered up your pennies. We are all ready. I shan't tell who I am going to hang my basket for—'t is somebody that will be pleased with it.

WHITE.   I am going to hang mine for grandpa; he is so good, and I know it will please him.

PINK.   *Grandpa!* He is an *old* man. Why don't you hang it for some boy that you like?

WHITE.   Grandpa isn't *old*. He has lived a great many years, but that don't make him old; and I like him better than I do any of the boys.

THOMAS.   That is a hard cut, Fairy. I wish I were grandpa.

WHITE.   Can 't I hang mine for grandpa?

TEACHER.   To be sure you can, if you think it would give him pleasure.

WHITE.   I know it would. Bluey, who are you going to hang yours for?

BLUE.   'T is for some one that I like very much, but I had rather not tell here. Pinkey would only laugh at me. But he is a good boy, and he is sick.

THOMAS.   I wish I were a good boy and sick. My pennies are all picked up. Are we ready to commence our march?

TEACHER.   You are all ready, and I wish you a pleasant evening.   [*Exeunt.*

A GAME OF NUTS.

Characters:

BERTIE MAKEFUN.   ANNIE PLEASEALL.
NETTIE KINDHEART.   MINNIE INDOLENCE.
SALLY GRUMBLE.

NETTIE KINDHEART, sitting alone upon the stage.

[*Enter* BERTIE MAKEFUN.]

BERTIE. Nettie, what are you thinking of, here alone? I will exchange this handful of nuts for your last moment's thought. (*Offers the nuts.*)

NETTIE. Bertie, were your nut-shells all gold and the meat in them sugar and honey, I do not think I would make the trade.

BERTIE. Are your thoughts so precious then?

NETTIE. No, not precious, but too trifling and indefinite to be clothed in words.

BERTIE. Aunt Nancy says, everything that is worth doing at all, is worth doing well. She says, we should read well, work well, play well and think well. Now, I asked you for your thought, because I wanted to look at it a moment, to see if you thought well.

NETTIE. Look at my thought! That is a queer idea.

BERTIE. Well, we can look at thoughts as well as

211

anything else. There is only this difference — some things, your bouquet of flowers for an example, we look at with the natural eye. A thought we look at with the eye of the understanding. Now, Nettie, if you will give me the thought of this minute I will look at it and tell you what it is like.

NETTIE. My thought at this moment is, that Bertie Makefun is a queer girl.

BERTIE. Your thought, Nettie, is like a pure diamond.

NETTIE. I do not see the resemblance.

BERTIE. You are stupid. Your thought is like a pure diamond, because there is no alloy with it. You have stated a pure truth — I am a queer girl; I have a queer name; I was a queer baby. My mother says I laughed before I cried; and when I get hurt, I laugh now. O, there comes Minnie Indolence; lets get her thought.

[*Enter* MINNIE.]

Minnie, all these nuts for your last thought.

MINNIE. How many have you? If there is enough worth having, I will take them, and think I should get a good bargain.

BERTIE. (*Counting her nuts.*) There are eight; that is a great many; 't is two times four, according to Colburn's Mental Arithmetic; and I am sure they are worth having. Now give us your thought.

MINNIE. Well, Cousin Bertie, first the nuts. I 'll make sure of them, and also warn you, in time for you to retract you offer, that you are making a bad bargain.

BERTIE. (*Gives the nuts.*) I 'll take my chance for

that. Now speak honestly, and tell us what you were thinking of as you walked so leisurely along.

MINNIE. I saw a cunning little squirrel sitting on the fence sunning himself, and I thought if I were only a squirrel I should not have to go to school and study this dull spelling - book. And I should n't have to work at home either. You see, Bertie, you have made a poor bargain.

BERTIE. Not at all. Miss Indolence, your thought is in harmony with your name, and harmonies always satisfy. But then, squirrels have to work hard for the food they eat. Did you ever see them crack nuts with their sharp teeth? And how provident they are in providing for the cold winters. I do not think, Minnie Indolence, that you would be nimble enough for a squirrel; the cats would catch you and eat you up before you could get resolution enough to start on a race. But I see Annie Pleaseall coming. Minnie, please lend me your nuts that I may buy her thought. I will try to trade cheaper than I did with you; I will only give her half of them.

[MINNIE *gives the nuts. Enter* ANNIE.]
Annie, your last thought for half these nuts.

ANNIE. A bargain. (*Takes the nuts.*) I thought if I were only this beautiful rosebud (*holding one in her hand*), somebody — I mean every decent body — would love me.

BERTIE. Well, Annie Pleaseall, it would improve you somewhat to turn into a rosebud; you would then forget yourself, lose all desire for admiration, and become perfectly beautiful. Here is Sally Grumble

coming; these four nuts I'll offer her for her thought.
Now we shall get something rich.

[*Enter* SALLY, *poorly clothed.*]

Come, Sally, these four large nuts for your last thought.

SALLY. My last thought for four nuts! My thought
comes from much hard experience, and you, Bertie
Makefun, think to buy it for four nuts. You don't
trade with me that way, I assure you.

ANNIE. I will give you four more, Sally. Now give
us your thought; please do.

SALLY. I will not; no, I will not give my hard-
earned thought for four nuts, nor eight nuts, even to
Annie Pleaseall; and as for Bertie Makefun, I wouldn't
give one thought to her if her apron were full of nuts.

MINNIE. Well, Sally, how many nuts will you give
them to me for?

SALLY. How many nuts will I give them to you for,
Miss Indolence? If I should speak plainly to you, I
should say you would have to stir yourself early in the
morning to pick nuts enough in your lifetime to buy
one of my thoughts.

MINNIE. O, Sally, what have I done to merit such
severity?

SALLY. You have done *nothing*, Minnie; and this is
the charge I bring against you.

BERTIE. Well, Sally, there is Nettie; perhaps you
may be induced to trade with her.

SALLY. I might *give* them to Nettie Kindheart. She
never asked anything of me yet that I refused her.

NETTIE. This is very kind in you, Sally. Now, if
you please, give me your thought, and I will give you
mine in exchange.

SALLY. Whatever you ask, Nettie, I will give. I thought, and I think, this is a cold world we live in. Everything is turned topsy turvy. Winters are too cold, summers are too hot, spring too short, and autumn no better. Some people are too rich and some too poor; and you can't meet a poodle dog in the street, but you shudder at the thought that he may bite you.

BERTIE. You have given your kind friend, Nettie, many thoughts; which one shall I put into our morning journal?

SALLY. Every poodle dog may bite. Now, Nettie, give us your sunny thought; the world needs it.

NETTIE. Treat every poodle dog kindly, and they will have no teeth to bite with.

SALLY. One more thought on top of yours, Nettie. Sally Grumble would place her poor body between you and the veriest mad dog that walks on this sad earth.

[*They all clap their hands.*]

I don't say this of you, Bertie Makefun.

BERTIE. I know you do not, Sally. Your conduct speaks quite an opposite language to me. I never come into your presence without your growling. But I have not yet given my thought. As it is the last one, I suppose it should be the climax, Now, as we are all Homœopathists, and understand the philosophy of "like cures like," we can also understand this—grumble gets grumble.

[SALLY, *in a passion, leaves the stage.*]

NETTIE. O, Bertie, you are too severe on poor Sally. Her lot in life is cold. I am not sure if you had it to bear but some of your fun would be frozen into icicles.

Think of her poor, miserable home. Her mother died in her infancy; her wretched father is intemperate; and her Aunt Crossbar is quite worthy the name she bears. Sally gets little sunshine anywhere.

BERTIE. I know it, Nettie. Can't we give her some? Let's think of some funny surprise for her this Christmas evening.

ANNIE. So we will; and I'll tell you what will be nice. We will all look over our private drawers, and cull from our nicknacks there what we can spare; put them altogether into one bundle, and send them to Sally. This might give her a moment of sunshine

MINNIE. That is a happy thought, Annie. I have a great many things I would like to give away, and I propose that we send our things over to Nettie, and let her take them to Sally. She loves Nettie, you know; and it would increase the value of a present to receive it from her hands.

BERTIE. We ought first to enquire if Nettie would be willing to undertake so formidable a mission.

NETTIE. I should be delighted with the honor. I would walk ten miles to feel the warm glow from poor Sally's heart on receiving the gift of a "Christmas tree." I have got a cunning little tree at home that pa brought me; 't is so small I could carry it in my hand. Now, all the presents that we get together that would look pretty on the tree, I would hang on it; any larger ones I could put into a basket.

BERTIE. Admirable, your plan, Nettie. Let us hasten home to have things ready. We will send our budgets round to you. I shall put a bunch of fun inside of mine ; but do n't tell Sally who put it there, as it would make her ruffle up her stiff feathers.

[*Exeunt.*]

SCENE SECOND.

SALLY GRUMBLE, alone, with a large calico bag on her arm, well filled.

SALLY. Well, 't is a cold Christmas evening for all poor people ; 't is the frigid zone of the year. We feel the cold more now because everybody is so warm around us. My very soul shivers ; I am freezing ; I have no friend in this wide world to give me as much as a brass pin ; and this is n't the worst of it—I 've not a *friend* to give anything to. I will except Nettie Kindheart. This bag of nuts I gathered for her in the nut season. She will find the shells hard, but she can open them as she has the proud heart of the giver. If I had a mint of money, I would give it all to Nettie.

[*Enter* NETTIE, *with a beautifully dressed tree in one hand and a full basket in the other.*]

NETTIE. Sally, a bunch of friends have commissioned me to bring you this tree and basket. You will find them laden with many wishes for you, a merry Christmas.

SALLY. (*Drops her own bag and takes the gifts.*) I do not believe I have but one friend in the world, and to her I am very grateful. But a moment since I felt myself in the frigid zone, shivering with cold ; now I am transported to the torrid, and am melting with heat. (*Wipes her eyes.*) Nettie Kindheart, you keep green a small island in my cold desert-heart. All beside and all around it is a waste wilderness. Last year, in the season of nut-gathering, I spent the early mornings under the generous trees. Every nut they let fall I gathered for you. I have kept them for my Christmas offering. They are worth nothing, yet my lone heart is in them, and I know you will accept them, to please poor Sally.

NETTIE. Indeed I will, and thank you a thousand times. What a treat I shall have this winter! You must come over, Sally, and eat them with me. I have many pleasant things to tell you, and I have one very bright thought nestling itself warmly in the inmost of my heart: I shall tell it to you some of our nut-eating evenings. Would your Aunt Crossbar let you go away from her to live?

SALLY. Yes, and be thankful to have me. We live like two scratching cats tied together.

NETTIE. Well, Sally, you know I have no sister. I am going to talk to ma about something that will make us very happy. Good night; now I must hurry home.

[*Exit.*

SALLY. I have no voice for words; my throbbing heart is too full. I see a ray of summer light among the possibilities of the coming future. The world is not all a desert now. Nettie Kindheart has kept one tiny seed alive in this wintry heart of mine. I feel its throb; it may burst forth; it may live, grow, blossom and bear fruit. Sally Grumble may sleep one cold long night, then wake in the morning and find her name Grateful Sunshine.

[*Exit.*

THE KERNEL OF CORN.

Characters:

GEORGE LOWD,   LUCY CARLTON,
CHARLES BROWN, BESSIE REED.

CHARLES seated at a table, examining, with absorbing interest, the
contents of a small box. Books and papers on the table.

[*Enter* GEORGE, LUCY, *and* BESSIE, *in traveling dresses.*]

LUCY. I am so glad the evening is pleasant. I know
we shall have a delightful ride.

GEORGE. It is cold. Are you dressed warm?

LUCY. O, yes; I am wrapped up in furs. Ma
did n't like to have me go, but, after much coaxing,
she consented.

BESSIE. That was good in her. Your mother is
always so careful of you.

LUCY. You know I am the only girl mother has;
and although I may not make a mark in society, I make
my mark at home. The boys all say the sun has set,
when Lu is gone.

GEORGE. Tell your brothers, selfishness is a sin.
Other eyes beside theirs like to see the sun.

BESSIE. George is complimentary this evening, and
he can afford to be, for we have, to say the least, two

hours of pleasure before us — and a sleigh-ride in the evening, by moonlight, is a capital way to kill time.

CHARLES. (*In a loud voice.*) Murder! (*The others start.*)

GEORGE. What do you mean, Charles, by shouting in this way?

BESSIE. You frightened me half out of my senses.

CHARLES. That is well; you ought to be frightened. There is no merciful law to punish a criminal like you. If I can frighten you a little, it may do some good.

GEORGE. (*Throws his glove upon the table.*) I am the protector of these ladies this evening. We will meet in the morning.

CHARLES. (*Playfully returns the glove.*) I think you will need this before to-morrow morning. I will satisfy you for the offense I have given to-night, by throwing a ray of light upon the subject. Miss Bessie, here, is devising ways to *kill* time; and, if I see correctly, this is murder in the first degree, and we have no human law to punish it.

BESSIE. Charles, speak truly, now, does old Father Time never weigh your life down with a wearisome monotony?

CHARLES. Never.

GEORGE. I should judge, from your employment this evening, that you were trying to annihilate some of his leaden moments.

CHARLES. Not at all. I am filling the present with sweet memories of the past.

LUCY. While we are waiting for Sambo to bring our sleigh, let us see some of your curiosities.

CHARLES. (*Pushes towards her his box.*) With pleasure. They are all at your service.

BESSIE. What a variety you have, Charley. I could *kill* one hour, at least, in looking them over.

CHARLES. Do not, Bessie, talk of *killing time*. Every little moment of it is precious. I try to live in the present — to take each hour as it comes, and fill it full of life in some form. 'T is an old adage, but true, that a day lost is never found.

BESSIE. I do not see any sense in that old adage. I am not fond of adages, anyway.

CHARLES. You can see that time is ever onward — to-day goes and never returns. Our infancy will never come back to us ; the opportunity of growth to-day will not be ours to-morrow. So, I say, let us fill every little minute as it comes to us.

LUCY. Charles, would n't you have any pleasure in life ? Would you never go sleigh riding ?

CHARLES. Yes, I would go sleigh riding, and I have a great fancy for pleasure ; I love it so well that I try to fill *all time* with it. Activity of life in any right direction is pleasure to me.

LUCY. That 's my idea. I cannot tolerate indolence.

BESSIE. And I do not believe I am very partial to indolence. 'T is only when I have nothing to do that I feel murder in my heart — in other words, that I want to *kill* time.

CHARLES. Then, Bessie, why do n't you wake up to the great object of life, and try to grow into its perfections ?

BESSIE. I am awake, and, just now, interested in

your box of curiosities. What a medley you have here! Where did you get all this ancient coin?

CHARLES. From different sources. Grandfather gave me some of it.

BESSIE. This silver knee-buckle. I suppose there is some interesting legend connected with it.

CHARLES. I don't know of any. 'T is simply a family relic. It belonged to my great uncle.

BESSIE. (*Laughs.*) Well, a kernel of corn! This is a wonder! 'T is a marvelous curiosity! Look at it, George. Did you ever see anything like it?

GEORGE. I never saw anything like it.

LUCY. Now, George, what a big story for an honest boy to tell.

GEORGE. 'T is true. I never saw a distinguished kernel of corn before. Such a plebeian must have distinguished himself some way, to have knighthood conferred upon him. Please give us the history of his life, Charles?

CHARLES. With pleasure. You know my father's farm? 'T is one of the largest and best in the county.

GEORGE. Yes, we know this.

CHARLES. Well, this farm belonged to my grandfather.

GEORGE. And that we know. Now for the kernel of corn.

CHARLES. This farm, a few years ago, all lay in a kernel of corn.

GEORGE. That we didn't know. We have your word for it — and your word is good ; still, we should esteem it a great favor if you would give us some light on the 'subject.

CHARLES. My grandfather's parents died when he was a little boy, and left him and his grandmother alone and very poor. They struggled on a year or so with pinching poverty, then, to save themselves from starvation, they applied to the town for assistance. My grandfather was nine years old now; and when the charitable official called with his lumber cart to take them, in tender mercy, to the almshouse, the old lady burst into hysteric sobbing. When she could control herself, she said, "This is well for me — I sleep and wake — and all is over. I find a home where cold and hunger never come. But my child! He has just commenced life's journey — he is a good boy — spare him." The official kindly said, "I see he is a good boy; he is large and strong; he looks honest. I will take him home with me, and let him work on my farm, if you wish. He can feed the chickens now, and will soon be large enough to do more." The old lady accepted this offer with gratitude. When she was about parting with grandfather, she was distressed because she had nothing to give him. At last, she found in her pocket a kernel of corn. "God be praised," she said, " I have something! 'T is not the greatness of the gift that contains the blessing. My boy, take this — 't is your grandma's legacy — you will find a farm in it.

BESSIE. And is this the same kernel she gave him?

CHARLES. No; it is and it is n't. It is a descendant of it. 'T was autumn when grandpa received this wonderful legacy of a farm lying in a kernel of corn. He kept it, as something very sacred, until the sunny days of spring came, then he asked leave to bury it in one corner of the garden. "Grandma," he said, "is buried, and I will bury her last gift to me. If I keep it, I may lose it." He was delighted, in a few days, to see it shooting out of the ground a living thing. He watched it with great care and interest until the autumn days came round; then it was a large stalk, with three large ears of corn on it. He did his harvesting with manly pride. "*My farm*," he said; "grandma's gift." Next year he buried his three ears, and the next year, his three hundred; then he began to count his bushels — then tons; now he converted some of it into land — he had an acre. His kernel of corn kept growing — his acre enlarged; and now we see the farm.

GEORGE. Thank you, Charles, for enabling us to see for ourselves a farm in a kernel of corn. The humble little plebeian is worthy of knighthood.

CHARLES. Now a word for the *murderer* here. You see what a world lies hidden in this apparently insignificant kernel of corn.

BESSIE. I see it, Charles. It may multiply itself until it covers the whole habitable earth.

CHARLES. That is true; and the little minutes of time that you would kill, may be filled with some form of use that will multiply itself until it reaches eternity.

BESSIE. O, Charles, what a big thought you have given me to take sleigh riding!

LUCY. There is great truth in this thought. I feel it waking up some of my slumbering energies. He has planted a kernel of corn. I feel the tender germ springing into life. Next autumn we will look for the harvest.

CHARLES. If you guard the tender seedling well, I

know there will come a rich harvest; not only one, but another and another, even beyond human ken.

(*Sleigh bells are heard.*)

BESSIE. That is the sound. We do n't *kill* time when we enjoy it, do we? I will be a murderer no longer, for this sage philosopher to cry out against. Let us fill life to overflowing. The sleigh bells! there is music in them. Come, Charlie, go riding with us.

GEORGE. Yes, go; there is room. Quick! Sambo can 't hold the horses.

(CHARLES *picks up his treasures.*)

[*Curtain falls.*

THE POCKET-BOOK.

Characters:

MRS. DAVIS.   MR. ELLIS.
THOMAS LEE.   JOHN CARL.

[*Enter* THOMAS. *Hunts carefully over the carpet, moving chairs.*]

THOMAS. Auntie, have you seen my pocket-book anywhere here?

MRS. DAVIS. I did n't know that you had one.

THOS. Yes, I had. This morning, when I went into Mr. Ellis's store, I found one lying on the floor, near the door. I picked it up and put it into my pocket. Of course, it did n't belong to Mr. Ellis; he do n't keep his pocket-books in such a place.

MRS. D. Does it belong to you?

THOS. I should think it did. I found it.

MRS. D. Where did you say you found it?

THOS. On the floor.

MRS. D. Well, I found one, a few minutes ago, near the door, on this floor. I picked it up and put it in my pocket. I suppose, according to your reasoning, it belongs to me.

THOS. No, Auntie, it belongs to me; I found it first.

MRS. D. I do n't think it makes any difference who

found it first. I found it last, and 'have it in my possession, and I should think I had a better claim to it than you have.

THOS. No, you have n't; it belongs to me.

MRS. D. What claim have you on it? ˙

THOS. I found it.

MRS. D. So did I find it; but I do n't think it belongs to either of us. It has an owner, and you must try to find him.

THOS. How can I?

MRS. D. You can carry the pocket-book to Mr. Ellis; he will advertise it; and I have no doubt the owner will call for it. Here it is; run over with it as soon as you can, tell him where you found it, then leave it with him.

THOS. I do n't like to do it, Auntie. He will think I was dishonest to bring it home before I gave it to him.

[*A rap is heard at the door.*]

MRS. D. Open the door, Thomas.

[*Enter* MR. ELLIS.]

MR. ELLIS. Good evening, Mrs. Davis; good evening, Thomas.

THOS. Good evening. (THOMAS *starts to leave the room.*)

MR. E. Stop, my boy; I want to talk with you; my business here to-night is with you. I am in search of an honest boy.

THOS. I am not, then, the boy you want, sir.

MR. E. I am not sure of that. How old are you?

THOS. I am twelve years old, sir.

MR. E. Have you any brothers or sisters?

THOS. Not any. I have only a mother, and she is very poor. I go home nights to sleep, and I stay with auntie in the day, as I can be of a little use to her: then she says she likes my company. Mother do n't mind staying alone.

MR. E. If your auntie can spare you. I think you are the boy I want. I can afford to pay you something, and that will help your mother.

THOS. I do n't think I am the boy you want, sir.

MR. E. Would n't you like to work in my store? I want some one to carry small parcels, and remain in the store while I go home to dinner. I think you could wait on customers in small matters; you could sell matches and such nicknacks, could n't you?

THOS. Yes, sir; but I am not the boy you want.

MR. E. Would n't you like to work in my store? It would help your mother.

THOS. I should like it very much; and most of all, to help my poor mother. I suppose you would give her a half pound of tea sometimes; she likes it, but she does n't have any.

MR. E. I would give her all the tea she could drink, and all the sugar, coffee, fish, flour, and spices that she could use.

THOS. (*Embarrassed — stammers — then says*) Auntie will explain to you. I am not the *honest* boy you want. (*He starts to leave the room.*)

MRS. D. Stop, Thomas: do n't leave the room. I will explain all to Mr. Ellis. Give him the pocket-book, tell him where you found it, and that you were just going to take it over to his store.

THOS. (*Gives the pocket-book.*) I found it on the floor in your store this morning.

MR. E. (*Takes it.*) 'T is not mine; 't is a poor, worn thing, and has seen hard days. It must belong to some very poor child.

[*A rap is heard at the door;* THOMAS *opens it. Enter a ragged boy, crying.*]

BOY. Is Mr. Ellis here?

MR. E. I am Mr. Ellis. What is wanting?

BOY. (*Checks his sobs.*) I thought, maybe I lost my pocket-book in your store this morning. It held all the money I have; and I was going to buy my mother some medicine with it. She is very sick, and nobody to do anything for her but me.

MR. E. How much money did you have in your pocket-book?

BOY. I had twenty cents. 'T was a very old pocket-book; it was my mother's.

MR. E. (*Holding out the pocket-book.*) Does this look like the one you lost?

BOY. It is the one, sir; it is the very one. My name is John Carl; I live in D street, No. 6. If you will let me have my pocket-book, I will run for my mother's medicine. She is very sick. She is all the friend I have. I would die to save my mother from pain.

MR. E. You shall have your pocket-book, and I will put twenty cents more into it.

MRS. D. And I will add the same. (*Gives the money to* MR. E.)

THOS. I have got no money. My mother is poor, like yours. She is not sick. I will give you my jack-knife. (*Offers it to him.*)

Boy. Thank you, but I will not take it. My pocket-book, and I will run.

Mr. E. (*Gives it to him.*) When you have carried the medicine to your mother, come into my store.

Boy. Yes, sir; thank you; and thank you and the lady for the money. (*He hurries off.*)

Mr. E. Well, Thomas, I am in haste. How soon can you commence working for me?

Thos. Do you think I am honest enough for you?

Mr. E. You have the reputation of being a very honest boy. Are you not honest?

Thos. Am I honest, Auntie?

Mrs. D. You made a little mistake about the pocket-book. You thought, as you did not know the owner, it belonged to you; but I believe when the matter was shown to you in a clear light, your feelings were all right. I will stand responsible to Mr. Ellis for your entire honesty.

Mr. E. You will excuse me, Mrs. Davis, but I cannot accept you as security. I will take Thomas upon his own merits. I will trust him. All that I have in my store I shall daily leave in his entire charge while I am away to dinner, and sometimes on longer errands. Can you come to - morrow?

Thos. Yes, Mr. Ellis; and I will do everything for you that I can. I will come in the morning before daylight, if you want me; and I will stay late in the evening. O. my mother will be so much pleased! You will find me an *honest* boy, Mr. Ellis. I know all the Commandments; and mother teaches me to live them.

Mr. E. I have confidence in you, Tom. Come in the morning at eight o'clock. I must go; good night.

[*Exit.*

Thos. O, Auntie, I would give all I ever had if I had n't brought that poor boy's pocket-book home with me.

Mrs. D. It will be a good lesson to you; 't will teach you to be ever watchful of what you do. Watch yourself in small things; do not yield to a shadow of wrong in thought or action; be truthful always; be honest as the morning sun.

Thos. I will, Auntie. I will be as honest and truthful as the king of day. He never deceives us; he never steals from us. Sometimes the black cloud hides his light, but as soon as it passes away we see him still there, in all his brightness. How often mother has told me this; and I will run home and tell her of my good fortune.

Mrs. D. I will go with you. [*Exeunt.*

THE TANGLED THREAD.

Characters:

KITTIE EARL; MARY and DAISY EARL, *her Cousins; and* NELLIE THORP.

KITTIE, sitting in a chair, trying to disentangle a skein of thread; her two cousins on crickets beside her, playing with dolls.

[*Enter* NELLIE.]

NELLIE. What are you all doing here? Little cousins playing with dollies; and what are you doing, Kittie?

KITTIE. What am I doing? I am trying to pick out this snarl of thread. I am discouraged. I can never pick it out; and I have tried and tried, but it will never be smooth under my impatient fingers.

NELLIE. Try again.

KITTIE. I have, and the determined thing will not yield one inch of its fixings.

NELLIE. Try again, Kittie; never give up. If you find the snarl more and more complicated, redouble your perseverance.

> All that other folks can do,
> Why, with patience, may not you?
> Only keep this rule in view,—
> > Try again.

KITTIE. O, Nellie, do n't keep talking to me about trying again. I 'm out of patience.

NELLIE. There is your trouble — you have permitted yourself to get out of patience; your mind is in a snarl O, Kittie, who would have thought a simple skein of thread could cloud the sunshine of your mind!

KITTIE. And yet 't is true, this old thread has done it.

NELLIE. Did you ever read the story of Robert Bruce's sixth failure in attempting to free Scotland, and that watching the perseverance of a spider he was led to make the seventh attempt, which was successful? Now I suppose you have worked six seconds over that snarl; try the seventh one, and you will succeed.

KITTIE. I will try no more; the thing is n't worth such sacrifice of feeling. Little cousins may have it to fill pin-cushions for their dollies.

NELLIE. Well, Kittie, you will never excel in anything unless you learn patience and perseverance. This morning, when I was in the garden, I noticed a little bird picking up straws and sticks, to weave into her nest. Once she tried to fly to a tree with a stick in her bill too heavy for her to carry, and before she had quite reached her nest it fell to the ground. She was not discouraged; she patiently picked it up, and tried again. Again it fell. Was her patience exhausted? Not at all. I watched her with much interest. Five times she failed. I began to despair of her success. But the sixth was a complete victory; and I gave her such a loud cheer that I nearly frightened her away.

DAISY. I should like to see that little birdie.

MARY. If Day and I had been there we would help birdie carry the heavy stick. Would n't we, Day?

DAISY. Yes; and we would help her build her nest.

NELLIE. Little cousins, can 't you sing to Kittie that pretty song you know about the birds. (*They sing.*)

> I love to watch the little bird,
>   As patiently she weaves
> Her little nest upon the tree,
>   Half hid among the leaves.

KITTIE. That is a pretty little song, and I will be like the birds, and try my snarly thread again. But, Nellie, did you never try to do a thing and give it up? Did you never find a twig too heavy for you to carry?

NELLIE. Yes; I once tried to teach my dollie to sing, and my success was no better than that of the boy who tried to teach his pig to read. And I once tried to subtract ten from eight, and failed in the attempt.

DAISY. And I failed last night to keep my fingers warm when I was coasting. But, then, we had a good time, and did n't care if our fingers were cold; did we, May?

MARY. No, we did n't know they were cold until we got into the house, where the fire was. Day cried a little then.

KITTIE. That is a good lesson for me. If I can keep my mind from thinking about this snarl, I shall have it all done without knowing that it is such a draw on good nature. Little cousins, please sing me another song; this will help me as much as it would have helped little birdie had you carried straws for it to build its nest of.

NELLIE. Now, Kittie, this seems like doing something. When you make up your mind that you *will* do a thing, the work is half done. Come, little cozs, sing a song —

> What bird and bee and ant can do
> Our Kittie Earl can do it too.

MARY. What shall we sing about?

KITTIE. Sing me that pretty song of the daisies.

MARY.

> Art thou crazy,
> Little Daisy,
> Blooming out so late?
> Dost thou know
> That the snow
> Soon will seal thy fate?

DAISY.

> I'm not crazy,
> But good Daisy,
> Blooming out so late.
> Well I know
> That the snow
> Soon will seal my fate.
>
> But I care not,
> And I fear not,
> For I've tried to do
> All my duty
> Well and truly,
> With my end in view.
>
> He who gave me
> Youth and beauty
> Would not have me lie
> All inactive,
> Unattractive,
> Fearing lest I die.

MARY.

> Then I 'll praise thee,
> Little Daisy,
> For I 've learned of you
> A good lesson,—
> Still to press on
> Whatever may ensue.

KITTIE.   Thank you, little cousins. Your pretty song gave a charm to my work. The tangled thread is all smooth. While you were singing, I did n't know my fingers were *cold*.

NELLIE.   And they are not cold now, Kittie. The comparison between your work and the cousins' play is not quite perfect. They played first, and toiled afterwards in the warming of the frosty fingers. You toiled first in overcoming the difficulties; afterwards comes the satisfaction. Say, Kittie, do you not feel yourself an inch taller than you would be if you had given your thread to stuff pin-cushions with?

KITTIE.   I feel like a luscious peach — good all over. But I am indebted to you and the pets here for my success. Now work is done, I suppose we may play. Let 's run into the yard and see what will offer itself there. Bring dollies along with you.   [*Exeunt.*

SORROWING NETTIE.

Characters:

NETTIE, HATTIE, *and* KATIE.

(NETTIE *alone.*)

NETTIE.

I am alone — my heart is sad,
  No sisters dear have I ;
Mary, Lucy, and brother Ned,
  All in the cold grave lie.

I am alone — no one to love,
  No one to help me play ;
My Dolly, you are good for nought,
  You hear not what I say ;

You cannot give to me a kiss,
  You cannot even smile ;
Away, then, Dolly, go away,
  And lay you there awhile.

(*Enter* HATTIE.)

HATTIE.

Dear Cousin Nettie, why so sad?
  Why throw Dolly away?
What shadow hides your morning sun?
  Tell, O tell me, I pray.

237

NETTIE.

> I am alone — and, worse than this,
>   My loved ones all are dead ;
> Mary and Lucy long ago,
>   And now, dear brother Ned.
>
> Yes, brother Ned is in the grave,
>   Mary and Lucy, too ;
> My heart will break, I am so sad,
>   What can I ever do?

HATTIE.

> Look up, Nettie — and look around,
>   All sadness then will flee ;
> " Because I live, so thou shalt live,"
>   Our Saviour says to thee.
>
> Turn from the grave, then, Nettie, turn,
>   Your loved ones are not there,
> They are risen — and still they live —
>   List, and I'll tell you where.
>
> Lucy, Mary, and Cousin Ned,
>   With angels now do dwell,
> Their dust alone is in the grave,
>   Dear Nettie, " All is well."

NETTIE.

> I hear your words, but do not know
>   How they can live again ;
> I saw them die — their cold, clay forms —
>   O, how I trembled then !

HATTIE.

> A corn of wheat put in the ground,
>   Nettie, you know must die,
> Then up it springs — the blade, the ear —
>   Its heart cannot there lie.
>
> Your sisters live, and cousin Ned —
>   Nettie, I *know* they do ;
> " Because I live, so thou shalt live,"
>   Our Saviour says to you.

NETTIE.

How can they live ? So great a change
  I do not understand ;
They must be dead — I saw them die,
  And felt their cold, clay hand.

(Enter KATIE *with a butterfly.)*

KATIE.

Hattie ! Hattie ! O, look here !
  This butterfly — do see ;
How wonderful ! Its wings so bright —
  'T is a perfect beauty.

I took it from the ground a worm,
  Creeping beneath our feet ;
Who would have thought so vile a thing
  Could change to one so sweet !

HATTIE.

Yes, beautiful indeed it is,
  I 'm glad you brought it here ;
See its bright spots — its perfect shade —
  Let Nettie view it near.

Now, Nettie, look ! This butterfly,
  A creeping worm it was,
It wove itself a winding sheet,
  It *died* — then came forth thus.

Now you may say, " So great a change
  I do not understand ;"
But ne'er again, " Loved ones are dead,
  I felt their cold, clay hand."

" Because I live, so thou shalt live,"
  I hear our Saviour say ;
Help Thou dear Nettie's unbelief,
  Father, to Thee I pray.

NETTIE.

Hattie, your prayer to God is heard,
  I do — I must believe —
Still, I 'm alone, my heart is sad,
  I cannot help but grieve.

HATTIE.

Are you alone in this bright world,
  And sad with none to love?
Have you ne'er learned our Father's name
  Can you not look above?

"Little children," our Saviour said,
  "Must ever love each other;
Each must be a sister kind,
  Each a loving brother."

O, Nettie, sisters all are we,
  One Father kind is ours;
Do you not feel His warming love?
  See beauty in His flowers?

NETTIE.

Yes, I do see and feel love now,
  I am not all alone —
Sisters and brothers we must be —
  I love you, every one.

(All sing.)

Sisters and brothers all are we,
  One love unites us all;
"Our Father," every day we 'll say,
  "Do keep us, lest we fall."
Then, sisters, brothers, all are we,
  One Father kind is ours;
We 'll keep His word, he then will strew
  Our pathway o'er with flowers.

WHAT CHRISTMAS MEANS.

𝕮𝖍𝖆𝖗𝖆𝖈𝖙𝖊𝖗𝖘:

KITTIF COLD, LULIE DAY, SUSIE BARNES, ROSIE LEE, LILLIE BATES,
and four little girls with their Teacher.

KITTIE alone.

KITTIE. What a great meaning Christmas has! And Christmas-day is the greatest day in the year. It means give — give — give! Many years ago our Saviour came into the world, and *gave* His life to save the people from sin and sorrow. The sun *gives* his bright light and warm beams to gladden our earth. The black cloud which sometimes frightens us with its terrific thunderbolts *gives* the grateful raindrops to refresh the thirsty and drooping plant. The earth *gives* abundantly. And what beautiful presents Christmas trees give to almost every body. And poor Kittie Cold, with her ragged dress and worn-out shoes, has nothing to give. She can't be Christmas.

[*Enter* LULIE.]

LULIE. Are you sure of that, Kittie? Quite sure you have nothing to give?

KITTIE. I did n't know you were listening to me, Lulie. I thought I was alone, and was just going to ask the fairies to give me riches, so that I could be Christmas; then I would plant Christmas trees for all the poor people. But wishing and asking don't amount to anything. I am only poor Kittie Cold, with nothing to give.

LULIE. Are you sure of that Kittie? Have you nothing to give?

KITTIE. Why, yes, I have a *little* to give. I have a penny in my pocket, and I am going to give it to Sally Creeper. I don't suppose she ever had a penny in her life. You know she is poorer than I am, for she has no mother; she has a father, but he is very cross, and her Aunt Betty scolds her from morning till night. I have been keeping this penny two months, that I might have something to give at Christmas. I wish I had more. I should like to plant a tree at every corner of the street, and hang its branches full of shoes and warm dresses for poor children. But how came you to know, Lulie, that I had anything to give? How did you know I had this penny in my pocket?

LULIE. I didn't know that you had a *penny;* but I did know that a girl with a heart as warm as yours had something to give at Christmas.

KITTIE. Well, 'tis strange that you should know I had anything to give. I have kept this penny a secret ever since Blind Oliver gave it to me. Only mother knew it. I couldn't keep it all to myself; it was too good; and when I told her she was as pleased as I was, because I had something to give at Christmas. I am going round by Sally's house when I go home. But, Lulie, how came you to know poor Kittie Cold had anything to give?

LULIE. I saw through your ragged dress and worn shoes that you were rich.

KITTIE. Rich! Me rich, Lulie!

LULIE. Yes, Kittie Cold is rich; she is rich in a warm, generous heart.

KITTIE. Ah well! however warm and generous my heart may be, I have only one cent to give at Christmas. And this is better than nothing. Poor Sally will be pleased with it.

LULIE. Kittie, do you not know there are many other things to give beside money?

KITTIE. O yes, indeed; there are books, and pictures, and dresses, and shoes, and mittens, and everything.

LULIE. And do you not know you give every day what is better than all these presents?

KITTIE. Me give? no. What do I give?

LULIE. Our teacher says you are one of her best pupils, because you *give* such attention to your lessons; and she says you *give* attention to everything she says to you.

KITTIE. Well, I should n't suppose there was anyone so poor that they would not give these things.

LULIE. Our teacher says there is one thing that you might give her that you never do.

KITTIE. What is it? I am sure I mean to give her all I can. What does Miss Carey say I do n't give her?

LULIE. Trouble.

KITTIE. And who would give her *trouble?* I *would not.* If I have n't good things to give, I would n't give bad ones. I wish I had other things to give; and I wish I could give to somebody else beside our teacher.

LULIE. You give obedience to your mother every day, and this makes her happier than if you gave her millions of money.

KITTIE. You do n't think I would *disobey* my dear mother, do you, Lulie? I love her too much for this. But truly, I do wish I had something to give to everybody.

LULIE. And you have, dear Kittie: you have a smile for everybody, and a pleasant answer for every one that speaks to you. 'T is very few that are as rich in these Christ-gifts as you are. I have brought a little present to you. (*Gives her a package.*) Would you like it?

KITTIE. Thank you, Lulie. I can say I would like it before I open it, for I like everything. I never had many presents. O, 't is a pair of shoes; what nice ones they are!

LULIE. I do n't know as they will fit you; I did n't know what size you wear.

KITTIE. O, they 'll fit me fast enough. See here, (*holding up her mother's great worn-out shoes,*) any shoe fits me if it is n't too small.

[*Enter* SUSIE.]

SUSIE. A merry Christmas, dear Kittie. I have brought you a little present; I think you 'll like it; do you?

KITTIE. (*Opens the parcel.*) Now, Susie, this is too much. A nice warm dress! I thank you. Warm dress and shoes. I must have my name changed; I shall not be Kittie *Cold* now, but Kittie Warm. It makes me feel warm to look at them.

[*Enter* ROSA.]

ROSA. Will Kittie Cold accept a warm hood, to keep her ears from Jack Frost's fingers?

KITTIE. Dear me! I was never so pleased in all my life. How good you are, Rosa; how good you all are.

[*Enter* LILLIE.]

LILLIE. Kittie, I brought you a cloak; will you accept it?

KITTIE. O, what a Christmas has come down from heaven? What will my dear mother say when I go home?

[*Enter four little girls, with presents. They give them to* KITTIE.]

KITTIE. O, how much! how much! what shall I do? All these things 'most make me cry for joy. Will you let me give some of them to poor Sally Creeper?

[*Enter* GERTIE, *and crowns* KITTIE *with a wreath.*)

GERTIE. Kittie shall be Queen of Christmas.

KITTIE. O dear! gracious! what shall I do? Carry me away somewhere.

LULIE. (*Putting her arm around her.*) We will carry our queen into her room of state.

[*Enter* TEACHER, *with a basket.*]

TEACHER. I have heard our Kittie was to be made queen of the day, so I have brought her round a basket of convertibles that she may distribute among her poor subjects.

KITTIE. The fairies are all here. I asked them this morning to help poor Kittie *Cold.* They have done more than help her — they have made her rich Kittie

Warm.   A queen was never so grateful.   (*Picks up the basket.*)   Thank you all.   I must go on my blessed mission — must seek out my poor subjects. I am Christmas.   [*Exit.*

LULIE. This is the best Christmas I ever had. *Happy Kittie !*

THREE WAYS OF KEEPING CHRISTMAS.

Characters:

WALTER,	CHARLOTTE,
ROSIE,	MARY, *her Sister.*
LILLIE,	

CHARLOTTE sits with a book in her hand.

[*Enter* ROSIE, LILLIE, *and* MARY.]

ROSIE. Well, Miss Charlotte, I have had a merry Christmas. Mr. John Day wished me a merry one early this morning, just as the sun was rising; and a merry one I've had. My heart has danced the live-long day. I have had some presents, but so much play, and so many good things to eat, I am really tired, and ready to say "good night" to Christmas, and hie away to bed, for my limbs ache, not to mention my poor head. Have you had a merry time, Cousin Lillie?

LILLIE. No, Rosie; but I have had what grandpa says is better. I have had a happy Christmas — all day long. I have been as busy as the bee that makes our sweet honey. I was up this morning at the first crowing of the cock; but mother was earlier, and, before I

247

was dressed, she opened my door and said, " A happy Christmas to my daughter." And then she laid upon my table a new book, with many Christmas stories in it, and I have been reading them to grandpa, and talking with him all day. You know he is almost blind, and cannot read himself, and he likes to hear me read. Then he explains things to me that I do n't understand; and to-day he told me the story of a little boy he once knew; his name was Nathan. Grandpa said every day in the year was *Christmas* to Nathan—he was happy all the time, and always trying to be good and do good.

ROSIE. Well, I should n't want every day in the year to be Christmas, I am so tired.

CHARLOTTE. I think you would n't, Rosie, if you spent them all as you have spent this one.

ROSIE. I have n't been wicked to-day, Miss Charlotte. I do n't think I have done one naughty act. I 've had a real merry Christmas — have played all day with my cousins, and when we did n't play, we were eating goodies; but my head aches bad enough to-night, and I want to go to bed.

CHARLOTTE. I am glad you have done no naughty act. Have you done any good one?

ROSIE. I do n't know as I have. I have n't thought about it.

CHARLOTTE. Have you tried to make anybody happy?

ROSIE. I guess not. I have tried to have a grand merry Christmas, and I have had one; and I am so tired, every bone in my body aches.

CHARLOTTE. Did you ever think, Rosie, what Christmas day means, and what we mean when we talk about celebrating it?

ROSIE. I never thought anything about it. I always try to have a good time when the day comes round.

CHARLOTTE. I think you would have a better time if you should think about it, and try to understand the meaning of it.

ROSIE. I am satisfied with what I have now — a real merry Christmas; but let us hear what kind of a day Mary has had, then I will shut my heavy eyelids for the night.

MARY. I have not had a *merry* day.

LILLIE. Perhaps you have had a happy one, which is better. I know you have enjoyed it some way, for your face is such a perfect tell-tale. Look at her, Miss Charlotte.

CHARLOTTE. Yes, we can read much in Mary's face; she always lets the spirit shine through it. She never seems to have anything to conceal. Now, a beautiful repose rests there; 't is the form of harmony. But we would like to hear of her day.

MARY. I have passed the whole day with my sick auntie. When she was too warm, I fanned her; when she was thirsty, I gave her drink. Sometimes I read to her, and sometimes she liked to hear me sing. She says my voice is just right for a sick room.

LILLIE. Well, I think, Mary, your day, like mine, has been a happy one.

MARY. It has n't been like yours, Lillie; but it has been very happy. I shall never forget it.

CHARLOTTE. I think Mary has had a peaceful Christmas.

LILLIE. Is not a peaceful Christmas a happy one?

CHARLOTTE. Yes, it includes happiness; but, as you said, a happy day is better than a merry one, I will add, a peaceful day is better than a happy one. But the three are all good, yet they rise one above the other — merriment, happiness, and peace. Mary has had a peaceful day.

MARY. O, yes, my Christmas has been full of peace, and I feel it all about me now. I am not tired; my head do n't ache; I 'm in no haste to go to sleep — I would rather go and sit beside auntie's bed again; but I left her because the nurse came.

LILLIE. What made you so peaceful there? Sometimes I think it is dreadful lonely in a sick room.

MARY. You would n't find it so in Aunt Sadie's room. 'T is light there, and she talks so pleasantly to you. She gave me that nice music-box of hers; and when I said, " Aunt Sadie, you will want it when you get well." She smiled, and said, " No; I expect when I get well I shall have a better one." Then she told me about heaven; she said it was not a great way off, but all about us here. She said it was in the heart of every good person, and every good child had heaven with them. I like to hear Aunt Sadie talk. I think it was her pleasant conversation that gave me a peaceful Christmas. Was n't it, Charlotte?

CHARLOTTE. Partly that, Mary; but had not your heart been right, all that she said would not have brought you peace. Your act of self-denial — in other words, your sacrifice of personal gratification to duty in the early morning — prepared you for all that you have received. Had you accepted the invitation of your young friends, and gone sleigh riding, instead of staying with sick auntie, you might have had a merry day, but it would not have been a peaceful one.

LILLIE.   Is it wrong, Miss Charlotte, to go sleigh riding on Christmas?

CHARLOTTE.   'T is not wrong, when the way is all open for you to enjoy it; but if you sacrifice some use or duty for the pleasure of the ride, you are selfish, and that is wrong.   We should try not to be selfish any day, and, least of all, Christmas.

[*Enter* WALTER.]

WALTER.   Good evening, ladies; I hope I am not an intruder.   I am sent here by that good old man, of whom you have all heard — that benevolent old gentleman who has been on this earth nearly nineteen hundred years, and who is wise above others.   He has the power of looking into the hearts of children — little and big ones — and there he sees just what they need.   Once a year, when Christmas comes round, he employs many carriers to distribute his presents.   To-day I am in his service, and am here to do his bidding.

CHARLOTTE.   You are welcome, sir.   Take a chair. We have n't the honor of knowing your name.

WALTER.   I do not wish to sit.   My name is of little moment.   I introduced myself, on first entering, as the servant of a famed old gentleman, of whom you have all heard.   This, I supposed, would be a passport; but since a lady's curiosity craves more, I will say, I am Discretion — but I have no time for words — moments fly.   I have many distributions to make.   (*Taking from his pocket a large jewsharp, he gives it to* ROSIE.)   A merry Christmas!   This will make music for you.

ROSIE. Thank you, Mr. Discretion. I do n't think this will discourse music that will be very entertaining to my friends.

WALTER. I presume not, but 't is a good thing to make merry over. (*He now presents* LILLIE *a handsomely-bound book.*) Will you accept a volume of Whittier's illustrated poems? 'T is a little in advance of your years, but you will soon grow to it; in the waiting time, grandpa will explain it to you.

LILLIE. O, many thanks, good Mr. Discretion. 'T is not above my years. I love "Maud Muller" now dearly, and "The Playmate" too.

WALTER. (*Takes a guitar from its covering, and presents it to* MARY.) Our friend Mary finds her home in music. This will be a gentle accompaniment to her gentle voice. It will not jar even a sick bed, but will breathe harmony from her light touch. Will she accept it?

MARY. My heart thanks you, kind sir. My voice is small, and needs help. Call round to my home, and I will sing you a song of gratitude.

WALTER. (*Now gives* CHARLOTTE *a large and elegantly-bound Bible.*) This gift needs no comments. Your mind is open to its light and life. No reply is needed. [*Exit.*

ROSIE. Well, this is a remarkable closing of Christmas. I am very tired and stupid to-night, yet I understand the lesson; 't is a good one. I will put my symbol under my pillow; perhaps I shall do something more than make merry over it. Good night. [*Exit.*

LILLIE. And I must go home and show grandpa my

present.   Good night.   We will never forget this
Christmas.   [*Exit.*

MARY.   O, sister Charlotte, how many things do
come to me just as I need them !   My voice is small.

CHARLOTTE.   But 't is very sweet, and full of
melody.

MARY.   Aunt Sadie says so ; but this guitar will
help it, and I think auntie will enjoy hearing me play
it.   How wonderfully things do come to us !   I am sure
there is a Providence watching us every moment.

CHARLOTTE.   Let me read from my beautiful present,
and then we must go home.   (*Opens to the twelfth
chapter of Luke, and reads.*)   " Consider the lilies, how
they grow ! they toil not, they spin not ; and yet, I say
unto you, that Solomon in all his glory was not arrayed
like one of these.   If then, God so clothe the grass,
which is to-day in the field, and to-morrow is cast into
the oven ; how much more will He clothe you, O ye of
little faith ? "

MARY.   Yes, sister, He will clothe us, for He takes
care of the tiny sparrows.   We will fear nothing.   Let
us go home, and I will chant the Lord's Prayer, and
play a very gentle accompaniment.   [*Exeunt.*

A SUBSTANTIAL CHRISTMAS WISH.

Characters:

MARY DAY.   LULIE CASE.
ALICE BENT.   GEORGE DOW.

MARY, sitting alone.

[*Enter* LULIE.]

LULIE.   I wish you a merry Christmas, May.

MARY.   Thank you, Lulie.   I was just going to wish poor Mrs. Dayton one.

LULIE.   Poor Mrs. Dayton!   She lives two full miles from here.   You are not going to tramp all that way to wish that poor woman a merry Christmas, are you? What have you got in your basket?   May I take a peep?

MARY.   Yes, you may take a peep.

LULIE.   Dear me!   A whole chicken, an apple pie, and a large pudding.   You are not going to lug this heavy load up those long hills?

MARY.   I do not expect to find the load heavy nor the hills long.   The very thought of the poor woman's joy on receiving these goodies will lighten the basket

254

and shorten the way. 'T would be but mockery to go and wish her a merry Christmas on a crust of bread and dry bones. Grandpa says, if we would have our wishes really worth anything, we must make them substantial.

LULIE. Well, your wish is substantial enough — chicken, pie and pudding.

[*Enter* ALICE.]

ALICE. I wish, May, I had a basket twice as heavy as yours, and I would go along with you. I would walk up those long hills any time to see Mrs. Dayton's eyes sparkle when she is pleased.

MARY. I wish you *would* go with me, Alice ?

ALICE. I would had I not engaged to make a Christmas wreath for sister. I must hasten home, or I shall not get it done. But, May, let me put this apron in your basket for the good woman. I made it for Susan Jones, but she has aprons enough ; besides, she will have her hands full of presents, and will never miss mine. I would rather give it to poor Mrs. Dayton.

MARY. Thank you, Alice. I am pleased to have it added to the little parcel I have. I will give it to Mrs. Dayton from you, with your good wishes.

ALICE. That is right. She remembers me. I have been to see her many times. I would walk up those hills just to hear her talk. I know what she will say to you this morning. After invoking Heaven's blessing on your head for the nice present you carry her, she will tell you that delightful story she so likes to dwell on at Christmas. She always tells it in her own interesting way. It is ever fresh from her lips. How many times I have heard her repeat it

LULIE. If you have heard her repeat it so many times, will you not tell it to me?

ALICE. I would tell it to you, but I could not give the charm to it she does. We have all read the story many times; but we must hear her tell it to appreciate it.

LULIE. Please tell it to me, Alice; you have a good memory, and are a good imitator too.

ALICE. I will do the best I can. Let me think a moment how she commences. This is the way:— " That must have been a delightful country where the shepherds remained all night in the field, guarding their sheep and lambs. How tender and faithful those good shepherds were! I often wonder if these were the only people on earth good enough to see the rejoicing angels when our Saviour was born. O, how tenderly our Heavenly Father loves us! The angel of the Lord came upon those good shepherds, and the glory of the Lord shone round about them, and they were frightened. Do you not think it strange they were frightened?" Here the good old lady always pauses for an answer; and I will do the same. Lulie, do you think it strange the good shepherds were frightened?

LULIE. No, I don't think it strange. I should be frightened out of my senses were I to see an angel.

ALICE. Then you must never go to see Mrs. Dayton, for her house is full of them.

LULIE. And you may be sure I never will, if her house is haunted.

MARY. Who ever thought of good Mrs. Dayton's house being haunted?

ALICE. No one but Lulie. I should never call a house haunted that was so pure and holy that heaven's angels could dwell in it.

LULIE. How do you know angels are there? Do you ever see them?

ALICE. I do not see them; I have not eyes for such pure seeing. Laura Bridgeman, you know, has not eyes to see persons in this world. But Mrs. Dayton says they are there, and she says that is the reason she never feels alone. And I suppose that is the reason she is always so happy too. For there must be something that we do n't see to make such a poor, lame and almost blind woman always happy.

MARY. Alice, please go on with the story, for it is getting late.

ALICE. " And the angel said unto the good shepherds, fear nothing, for I bring you only joyful tidings. To-day, in Bethlehem, is born a precious babe, and He is to be called a Prince, Councellor, the Mighty One, Hero! These are great names, but a dearer one is added — He is our Saviour. This happened more than eighteen hundred years ago, and yet, in these present days, this same Saviour is born again in our hearts. He is born there when we keep all His sayings, when we speak truth and do good. But if we speak falsely and do evil, we crucify Him. The possibility of doing this wicked deed is fearful to think of. We need to watch ourselves very closely, lest we in some way hurt the tender babe that is born in us. Did you ever think of this, my little friend?" You must answer me, Lulie. Did you ever think of it?

LULIE.   No.

ALICE.   You must answer the questions, or else I can't go on.   Mrs. Dayton always waits for an answer. Do you love the Saviour?

LULIE.   Go on with the story, and not keep asking questions.   I cannot answer them.   I don't know.

ALICE.   Here is the test — " If ye love me, keep my commandments."   You have but to watch yourself to know if you keep the commandments.

LULIE.   Well, I have n't time for this watching, and I would n't much like it either.

MARY.   There is another test she sometimes gives — do you love your neighbor as yourself?

LULIE.   No, I don't.

[*Enter* GEORGE.]

GEORGE.   Excuse this interruption.   I have n't been a sly listener, but I could n't help hearing your conversation, for you have been talking very loud.   Lulie, did you ever read Keats' beautiful poem " Abou Ben Adhem "?

LULIE.   No.   If it has any relation to Mrs. Dayton's story, will you repeat it to us?

GEORGE.   If Alice will not think me intruding.

ALICE.   Indeed I will not ; please repeat it.

GEORGE.   " Abou Ben Adhem (may his tribe increase)
Awoke one night from a sweet dream of peace,
And saw within the moonlight in his room,
Making it rich, and like a lily in bloom,
An angel, writing in a book of gold.
Exceeding peace had made Ben Adhem bold;
And to the presence in the room he said,

'What writest thou?' The vision raised its head,
And with a look made of all sweet accord,
Answered, 'The names of those who love the Lord.'
'And is mine one?' said Abou. 'Nay, not so,'
Replied the angel. Abou spake more low,
But cheerily still; and said, 'I pray thee, then,
Write me as one that loves his fellow-men.'
The angel wrote and vanished. The next night
It came again, with a great wakening light,
And showed the names whom love of God had blessed,
And lo, Ben Adhem's name led all the rest."

I think Mrs. Dayton's name would follow close to Ben Adhem's; do n't you, Mary?

MARY. I would not be surprised if it took the lead even of his name.

GEORGE. If Alice will finish her story and allow me to remain a listener, I promise not to interrupt with any more poems.

ALICE. "Well, then, with the angel there came a heavenly host, praising God, and saying, 'Glory to God in the highest, and on earth peace and good will to man.' When this song of praise was ended, the good shepherds went to Bethlehem and found the babe. And the wise men from the East came also to see this precious babe; and they knelt down and worshipped Him. And they gave Him gold, frankincense and myrrh." She always closes her story in this way: "My little friends, we cannot see that holy babe, and He is not that babe now; He is our Saviour. We cannot give unto Him gold, yet we can give Him *what is better—a loving and obedient life*." You have the story, poorly told. To feel the tear start, you must hear it from Mrs. Dayton. Now I must hasten home to make sister's wreath. Good night. [*Exit.*

MARY. And I, too, must hurry on with my basket of merry Christmas.

GEORGE. Stop a minute, Mary; let me put this handful of pennies into your basket.

MARY. Thank you, George; they will buy the good woman some tea. Good night. [*Exit.*

GEORGE. I have my work to do, and so must say "good night" too. [*Exit.*

LULIE. Well, here I am, left alone. I 've no Christmas work to do; my hands are empty and my heart cold. Another Christmas shall not find me thus. I will do something for somebody. Grandma says, whenever you begin to do kind things for people you begin to love them. Ben Adhem's name was written first among those that love the Lord because he loved his fellow - men. I will do something. Lulie Case will have her name written somewhere. [*Exit.*

A CHRISTMAS ADDRESS.

DEAR FRIENDS,

Once more are we privileged to meet beneath these beautiful trees, richly laden with the golden fruits of affection, to bear love offerings and peace offerings to each other, and to unite our hearts in the glad song of a

WELCOME TO CHRISTMAS.

Christmas! The best day in the whole year. It awakens in the memory so many pleasant associations and grateful recollections. The past is richly spread out before us. Its leaves unfold until they reach our cradle-life. Love's mementos are written on every page. And "I wish you a Merry Christmas" is the melodious echo of each coming year.

I have said, the leaves of the past unfold till they reach our cradle-life. But may we not say they roll backwards much farther, even to those days when shepherds were in the field, keeping watch over their flocks by night? Suddenly a bright light appeared in the sky. 'T was strange and startling. The shepherds were afraid. Then, by their side, stood a loving angel, assuring their hearts and bidding them fear nothing; for, said the angel, "in the city of David is born this day a Saviour, who is Christ the Lord."

On the same night, wise men from the East saw a star. And they followed it until it stood over where the young child was. They were delighted on finding the babe, and they presented Him gold, frankincense and myrrh. After He had passed through the states of infancy and childhood, He commenced working those strange miracles which led the people to exclaim, " Thou art indeed the Christ, the Son of God."

Our Saviour remained clothed with a natural body a few of our short years, and then left it, saying, " I go that I may come again to you." Again He comes, but not as before. 'T is now a spiritual coming. He comes in the still, small voice that whispers of justice, mercy and peace. He comes in love. He comes with heaven's blessings into the hearts of all those who keep His commandments. He said then, He says now, and always, " Little children, love one another."

These trees, so richly laden with the golden fruit of affection, encourage us to believe He is now in our midst; that love is in our hearts; and that we do indeed love one another.

www.ingramcontent.com/pod-product-compliance
Lightning Source LLC
Chambersburg PA
CBHW031358020726
47499CB00005B/1449